Joel C. Harris

Mr. Rabbit at Home

A sequel to Little Mr. Thimblefinger and his queer country

Joel C. Harris

Mr. Rabbit at Home
A sequel to Little Mr. Thimblefinger and his queer country

ISBN/EAN: 9783337228064

Printed in Europe, USA, Canada, Australia, Japan

Cover: Foto ©Andreas Hilbeck / pixelio.de

More available books at **www.hansebooks.com**

MR. RABBIT AT HOME

A SEQUEL TO

Little Mr. Thimblefinger and his Queer Country

BY

JOEL CHANDLER HARRIS

AUTHOR OF "UNCLE REMUS," ETC.

ILLUSTRATED BY OLIVER HERFORD

BOSTON AND NEW YORK
HOUGHTON MIFFLIN COMPANY
The Riverside Press Cambridge

CONTENTS.

LIST OF ILLUSTRATIONS.

MR. RABBIT AT HOME.

I.

BUSTER JOHN ALARMS MR. RABBIT.

WHEN Buster John and Sweetest Susan and Drusilla returned home after their first visit to Mr. Thimblefinger's queer country, a curious thing happened. The children had made a bargain to say nothing about what they had seen and heard, but one day, when there was nobody else to hear what she had to say, Sweetest Susan concluded to tell her mother something about the visit she had made next door to the world. So she began and told about the Grandmother of the Dolls, and about Little Mr. Thimblefinger, and all about her journey under the spring. Her mother paid no attention at first, but after awhile she became interested, and listened intently to everything her little daughter said. Sometimes she

looked serious, sometimes she smiled, and some·
times she laughed. Sweetest Susan could n't
remember everything, but she told enough to
astonish her mother.

"Darling, when did you dream such nonsense
as that?" the lady asked.

"Oh, it was n't a dream, mamma," cried Sweet·
est Susan. "I thought it was a dream at first,
but it turned out to be no dream at all. Now,
please don't ask brother about it, and please don't
ask Drusilla, for we promised one another to say
nothing about it. I did n't intend to tell you,
but I forgot and began to tell you before I
thought."

A little while afterward Sweetest Susan's mother
was telling her husband about the wonderful im-
agination of their little daughter, and then the
neighbors got hold of it, and some of the old
ladies put their heads together over their teacups
and said it was a sign that Sweetest Susan was
too smart to stay in this world very long.

One day, while Drusilla was helping about the
house, Sweetest Susan's mother took occasion to
ask her where she and the children went the day
they failed to come to dinner.

"We wuz off gettin' plums, I speck," replied Drusilla.

"Why, there were no plums to get," said the lady.

"Well, 'm, ef 't wa'n't plums, hit must 'a' been hick'y nuts," explained Drusilla.

"Hickory nuts were not ripe, stupid."

"Maybe dey wa'n't," said Drusilla stolidly; "but dat don't hinder we chilluns from huntin' 'em."

"You know you did n't go after hickory nuts, Drusilla," the lady insisted. "Now I want you to tell me where you and the children went. I 'll not be angry if you tell me, but if you don't" —

Drusilla could infer a good deal from the tone of the lady's voice, but she shook her head.

"Well, 'm," she said, "we went down dar by de spring, an' down dar by de spring branch, an' all roun' down dar. Ef we warn't huntin' plums ner hick'y nuts, I done fergot what we wuz huntin'."

Drusilla seemed so much in earnest that the lady did n't push the inquiry, but when she went into another room for a moment, the negro girl looked after her and remarked to herself: —

"I done crossed my heart dat I would n't tell,

an' I ain't gwine ter. Ef I wuz ter tell, she would n't b'lieve me, an' so dar 't is ! "

Sweetest Susan was careful to say nothing to Buster John and Drusilla about the slip of the tongue that caused her to tell her mother about their adventures in Mr. Thimblefinger's queer country; but she did n't feel very comfortable when Drusilla told how she had been questioned by her mistress.

" Ef somebody ain't done gone an' tol' 'er," said Drusilla, " she got some mighty quare notions in 'er head."

Buster John, who had ideas of his own, ignored all this, and said he was going to put an apple in the spring the next day and watch for Mr. Thimblefinger.

" Well, ef you gwine down dar any mo'," remarked Drusilla, " you kin des count me out, kaze I ain't gwine 'long wid you. I 'm one er deze yer kind er quare folks what know pine blank when dey done got nuff. I been shaky ever since we went down in dat ar place what wa'n't no place."

" You will go," said Buster John.

" Huh ! Don't you fool yo'self, honey ! You can't put no 'pen'ence in a skeer'd nigger."

"If you don't go, you 'll wish you had," said Buster John.

"How come?" asked Drusilla.

"Wait and see," replied Buster John.

The next morning, bright and early, Buster John put an apple in the spring. He watched it float around for awhile, and then his attention was attracted to something else, and he ran away to see about it. Whatever it was, it interested him so much that he forgot all about the apple in the spring, and everything else likely to remind him of Mr. Thimblefinger's queer country.

Buster John went away from the spring and left the apple floating there. No sooner had he gone than one of the house servants chanced to come along, and the apple was seized and appropriated. The result was that neither Mr. Thimblefinger nor Mrs. Meadows saw the signal.

Buster John, thinking the apple had remained in the spring for some hours, waited patiently for two or three days for Mr. Thimblefinger, but no Mr. Thimblefinger came. Finally the boy grew impatient, as youngsters sometimes do. He remembered that the bottom of the spring, with the daylight shining through, was the sky of Mr.

Thimblefinger's queer country, and he concluded to give Mrs. Meadows and the rest a signal that they could n't fail to see. So, one morning, after water had been carried to the house for the cook, and the washerwoman's tubs had been filled, Buster John got him some short planks, carrying them to the spring one by one. These he placed across the top of the gum, or curb, close together, so as to shut out the light. Then he perched himself on a stump not far away, and watched to see what the effect would be. He knew he had the sky of Mr. Thimblefinger's queer country securely roofed in, and he laughed to himself as he thought of the predicament Mr. Rabbit would be in, dropping his pipe and hunting for it in the dark.

Buster John sat there a long time. Mandy, the washerwoman, got through with her task and went toward the house, balancing a big basket of wet clothes on her head and singing as she went. Sweetest Susan and Drusilla had grown tired of playing with the dolls, and were hunting all over the place for Buster John. They saw him presently, and came running toward him, talking and laughing. He shook his head and motioned toward the spring. They became quiet at once, and began to walk on their tiptoes. They seated themselves on the stump by Buster John's side, and waited for him to explain himself.

Presently Sweetest Susan saw the boards over the spring. "Oh, what have you done?" she cried. "Why, you have shut out the light! They can't see a wink. I don't think that's right; do you, Drusilla?"

"Don't ax me, honey," replied Drusilla. "I ain't gwine ter git in no 'spute. Somebody done gone an' put planks on de spring. Dar dey is, an' dar dey may stay, fer what I keer. I hope dey er nailed down."

"Please take the boards off," pleaded Sweetest Susan.

"No," said Buster John. "I put an apple in the spring the other day, and they paid no attention to it. Maybe they'll pay some attention now."

Suddenly, before anybody else could say anything, Drusilla screamed and rolled off the stump. Buster John and Sweetest Susan thought a bee had stung her. But it was not a bee. She had no sooner rolled from the stump than she sprang

to her feet and cried out, "Dar he is! Look
at 'im!"

Buster John and Sweetest Susan turned to
look, and there, upon the stump beside them,
stood Mr. Thimblefinger with his hat in hand,
bowing and smiling as politely as you please.

"I hope you are well," he said. Then he
began to laugh, as he turned to Buster John.
"You may think it is a great joke to come to the
spring, but it 's no joke to me. I have had a very
hard time getting here, but I just had to come.
Mrs. Meadows thinks there is a total eclipse going
on, and Mr. Rabbit has gone to bed and covered
up his head."

"How did you get here?" asked Buster
John.

"Through the big poplar yonder," said Mr.
Thimblefinger. "It is hollow from top to bottom, but it was so dark I could hardly find my
way. The jay birds used to go down through
the poplar every Friday until I put up the bars
and shut them out. I had almost forgotten the
road."

"Well," said Buster John, "I covered the
spring so that you might know we had n't forgot-

"HOW DID YOU GET HERE?"

ten you. I dropped an apple in the other day, but you paid no attention to it."

"I saw the apple," remarked Mr. Thimblefinger, "but it did n't stay in the spring long. It disappeared in a few minutes."

"Aha! I know!" exclaimed Drusilla. "Dat ar Minervy nigger got it. I seed her comin' long eatin' a apple, and I boun' you she de ve'y nigger what got it."

"Well, well!" said Mr. Thimblefinger. "It makes no difference now, and if you 'll get ready we 'll go now pretty soon."

"Why, I thought you could n't go down through the spring until nine minutes and nine seconds after twelve," suggested Buster John.

"The water gets wet or goes dry with the tide," Mr. Thimblefinger explained. "To-day we shall have to go at nineteen minutes and nineteen seconds after nine. It was nine minutes and nine seconds after twelve before, and now it is nineteen minutes and nineteen seconds after nine. Multiply nineteen by nineteen, add the answer together, and you get nothing but nines. You see we have to go by a system." Mr. Thimblefinger was very solemn as he said this. "Now, then,

come on.   We have n't any time to waste.   When
the nines get after us, we must be going.   There
are four of us now, but if we were to be multi-
plied by nine there would be nine of us, and nine
is an odd number."

"How would we be nine?" asked Buster John.

"It 's very simple," replied Mr. Thimblefinger.
"Nine times four are thirty-six.   Three and six
stand for thirty-six, and six and three are nine."

Buster John laughed as he ran to remove the
boards from the spring.   In a few moments they
were all ready in spite of Drusilla's protests, and
at nineteen minutes and nineteen seconds after
nine they walked through the spring gate into
Mr. Thimblefinger's queer country.

II.

Mrs. Meadows, Mr. Rabbit, Chickamy Crany Crow, and Tickle-My-Toes were very glad to see the children, especially Mrs. Meadows, who did everything she could to make the youngsters feel that they had conferred a great obligation on her by coming back again.

"I 'll be bound you forgot to bring me the apple I told you about," said she.

But Sweetest Susan had not forgotten. She had one in her pocket. It was not very large, but the sun had painted it red and yellow, and the south winds that kissed it had left it fragrant with the perfume of summer.

"Now, I declare!" exclaimed Mrs. Meadows. "To think you should remember an old woman! You are just as good and as nice as you can be!" She thanked Sweetest Susan so heartily that Buster John began to look and feel uncomfortable, — seeing which, Mrs. Meadows placed

her hand gently on his shoulder. "Never mind,"
said she, "boys are not expected to be as thought-
ful as girls. The next time you come, you may
bring me a hatful, if you can manage to think
about it."

"He might start wid 'em," remarked Drusilla,
"but 'fo' he got here he 'd set down an' eat 'em
all up, ter keep from stumpin' his toe an' spillin'
'em."

Buster John had a reply ready, but he did not
make any, for just at that moment a low, rumbling sound was heard. It seemed to come nearer
and grow louder, and then it died away in the
distance.

"What is that?" asked Mrs. Meadows, in an
impressive whisper.

"Thunder," answered Mr. Rabbit, who had
listened intently. "Thunder, as sure as you 're
born."

"Yes," said Mr. Thimblefinger. "I saw a
cloud coming up next door, just before we came
through the spring gate."

"I must be getting nervous in my old age,"
remarked Mrs. Meadows. "I had an idea that it
was too late in the season for thunder-storms."

"That may be so," replied Mr. Thimblefinger, "but it 's never too late for old man Thunder to rush out on his front porch and begin to cut up his capers. But there 's no harm in him."

"But the Lightning kills people sometimes," said Buster John.

"The Lightning? Oh, yes, but I was talking about old man Thunder," replied Mr. Thimblefinger. "When I was a boy, I once heard of a little girl " — Mr. Thimblefinger suddenly put his hand over his mouth and hung his head, as if he had been caught doing something wrong.

"Why, what in the world is the matter?" asked Mrs. Meadows.

"Oh, nothing," replied Mr. Thimblefinger. "I simply forgot my manners."

"I don't see how," remarked Mr. Rabbit, frowning.

"Why, I was about to tell a story before I had been asked."

"Well, you won't disturb me by telling a story, I 'm sure," said Mr. Rabbit. "I can nod just as well when some one is talking as when everything is still. You won't pester me at all. Just go ahead."

"Maybe it is n't story-telling time," suggested Mrs. Meadows.

"Oh, don't say that," cried Sweetest Susan. "If it is a story, please tell it."

"Well, it is nothing but a plain, every-day story. After you hear it you 'll lean back in your chair and wonder why somebody did n't take hold of it and twist it into a real old-fashioned tale. It 's old fashioned enough, the way I heard it, but I always thought that the person who heard it first must have forgotten parts of it."

"We won't mind that," said Sweetest Susan.

Mr. Thimblefinger settled himself comfortably and began : —

"Once upon a time — I don't know how long ago, but not very long, for the tale was new to me when I first heard it — once upon a time there was a little girl about your age and size who was curious to know something about everything that happened. She wanted to know how a bird could fly, and why the clouds floated, and she was all the time trying to get at the bottom of things.

"Well, one day when the sky was covered with clouds, the Thunder came rolling along, knocking at everybody's door and running a race with the noise it made; the little girl listened and wondered what the Thunder was and where it went to. It was n't long before the Thunder came rumbling along again, making a noise like a four-horse wagon running away on a covered bridge.

"While the little girl was standing there, wondering and listening, an old man with a bundle on his back and a stout staff in his hand came along the road. He bowed and smiled when he saw the little girl, but as she did n't return the bow or the smile, being too much interested in listening for the Thunder, he paused and asked her what the trouble was.

"'I hope you are not lost?' he said.

"'Oh, no, sir,' she replied; 'I was listening for the Thunder and wondering where it goes.'

"'Well, as you seem to be a very good little girl,' the old man said, 'I don't mind telling you. The Thunder lives on top of yonder mountain. It is not so far away.'

"'Oh, I should like ever so much to go there!' exclaimed the little girl.

"'Why not?' said the old man. 'The mountain is on my road, and, if you say the word, we 'll go together.'

"The little girl took the old man's hand and they journeyed toward the mountain where the Thunder had his home. The way was long, but somehow they seemed to go very fast. The old man took long strides forward, and he was strong enough to lift the little girl at every step, so that when they reached the foot of the mountain she was not very tired.

"But, as the mountain was very steep and high, the two travelers stopped to rest themselves before they began to climb it. Its sides seemed to be rough and dark, but far up on the topmost peak the clouds had gathered, and from these the Lightning flashed incessantly. The little girl saw the flashes and asked what they meant.

"'Wherever the Thunder lives,' replied the old man, 'there the Lightning builds its nest. No doubt the wind has blown the clouds about and torn them apart and scattered them. The Lightning is piling them together again, and fixing a warm, soft place to sleep to-night.'

"When they had rested awhile, the old man said it was time to be going, and then he made the little girl climb on his back. At first she did n't want the old man to carry her; but he declared that she would do him a great favor by climbing on his back and holding his bundle in place. So she sat upon the bundle, and in this way they went up the high mountain, going almost as rapidly as the little girl could run on level ground. She enjoyed it very much, for, although the old man went swiftly, he went smoothly, and the little girl felt as safe and as comfortable as if she had been sitting in a rocking-chair.

"When they had come nearly to the top of the mountain, the old man stopped and lifted the little girl from his back. 'I can go no farther,' he said. 'The rest of the way you will have to go alone. There is nothing to fear. Up the mountain yonder you can see the gable of the Thunder's house. Go to the door, knock, and do not be alarmed at any noise you hear. When the time comes for you to go, you will find me awaiting you here.'

"The little girl hesitated, but she had come so far to see where the Thunder lived that she would not turn back now. So she went forward, and soon came to the door of Mr. Thunder's house. It was a very big door to a very big house. The knocker was so heavy that the little girl could hardly lift it, and when she let it fall against the panel, the noise it made jarred the building and sent a loud echo rolling and tumbling down the mountain. The little girl thought, 'What have I done? If the Thunder is taking a nap before dinner, he 'll be very angry.'

"She waited a little while, not feeling very comfortable. Presently she heard heavy footsteps coming down the wide hall to the door.

"'I thought I heard some one knocking,' said a hoarse, gruff voice. Then the big door flew open, and there, standing before her, the little girl saw a huge figure that towered almost to the top of the high door. It wore heavy boots, a big overcoat, and under its long, thick beard there was a muffler a yard wide. The little girl was very much frightened at first, but she soon remembered that there was nothing for such a little bit of a girl to be afraid of.

"The figure, that seemed to be so terrible at first glance, had nothing threatening about it. 'Who knocked at the door?' it cried.

"Its voice sounded so loud that the little girl put her fingers in her ears.

SHE WAITED A LITTLE WHILE

"'Don't talk so loud, please,' she said. 'I 'm not deaf.'

"'Oh!' cried the giant at the door. 'You are there, are you? You are so small I did n't see you at first. Come in!'

"The little girl started to go in, and then paused. 'Are you the Thunder?' she asked.

"'Why, of course,' was the reply; 'who else did you think it was?'

"'I did n't know,' said the little girl. 'I wanted to be certain about it.'

"'Come in,' said the Thunder. 'It is n't often I have company from the people below, and I 'm glad you found me at home.'

The Thunder led the way down the hall and into a wide sitting-room, where a fire was burning brightly in the biggest fireplace the little girl had ever seen. A two-horse wagon could turn around in it without touching the andirons. A pair of tongs as tall as a man stood in one corner, and in the other corner was a shovel to match. A long pipe lay on the mantel.

"'There 's no place for you to sit except on the floor,' said the Thunder.

"'I can sit on the bed,' suggested the little girl.

"The Thunder laughed so loudly that the little girl had to close her ears again. 'Why, that is no bed,' the Thunder said when it could catch its breath; 'that 's my footstool.'

"'Well,' said the little girl, 'it 's big enough for a bed. It 's very soft and nice.'

"'I find it very comfortable,' said the Thunder, 'especially when I get home after piloting a tornado through the country. It is tough work, as sure as you are born.'

"The Thunder took the long pipe from the mantel and lit it with a pine splinter, the flame of which flashed through the windows with dazzling brightness.

"'Folks will say that is heat lightning,' remarked the little girl.

"'Yes,' replied the Thunder; 'farmers to the north of us will say there is going to be a drought, because of lightning in the south. Farmers to the south of us will say there 's going to be rain, because of lightning in the north. None of them knows that I am smoking my pipe.'

"But somehow, in turning around, the Thunder knocked the big tongs over, and they fell upon the floor with a tremendous crash. The floor appeared to give forth a sound like a drum, only a thousand times louder, and, although the little girl had her fingers in her ears, she could hear the echoes roused under the house by the falling tongs go rattling down the mountain side and out into the valley beyond.

"The Thunder sat in the big armchair smoking, and listening with legs crossed. The little girl appeared to be sorry that she had come.

"'Now, that is too bad,' said the Thunder. 'The Whirlwind in the south will hear that and come flying; the West Wind will hear it and come rushing, and they will drag the clouds after them, thinking that I am ready to take my ride. But it's all my fault. Instead of turning the winds in the pasture, I ought to have put them in the stable. Here they come now!'

"The little girl listened, and, sure enough, the whirlwinds from the south and the west came rushing around the house of the Thunder. The west wind screamed around the windows, and the whirlwinds from the south whistled through the cracks and keyholes.

"'I guess I'll have to go with them,' said the Thunder, rising from the chair and walking around the room. 'It 's the only way to quiet them.'

" 'Do you always wear your overcoat?' the little girl asked.

" 'Always,' replied the Thunder. 'There 's no telling what moment I 'll be called. Sometimes I go just for a frolic, and sometimes I am obliged to go. Will you stay until I return?'

" 'Oh, no,' the little girl replied; 'the house is too large. I should be afraid to stay here alone.'

" 'I am sorry,' said the Thunder. 'Come and see me get in my carriage.'

"They went to the door. The whirlwinds from the south and the winds from the west had drawn the clouds to the steps, and into these the Thunder climbed.

" 'Good-by,' he cried to the little girl. 'Stay where you are until we are out of sight.'

"There was a flash of light, a snapping sound, a rattling crash, and the Thunder, with the clouds for his carriage and the winds for his horses, went roaming and rumbling through the sky, over the hills and valleys."

Mr. Thimblefinger paused and looked at the children. They, expecting him to go on, said nothing.

"How did you like my story?" he asked.

"Is it a story?" inquired Buster John.

"Well, call it a tale," said Mr. Thimblefinger.

"Hit 's too high up in de elements for ter suit me," said Drusilla, candidly.

"What became of the little girl?" asked Sweetest Susan.

"When the Thunder rolled away," said Mr. Thimblefinger, "she went back to where the old man was awaiting her, and he, having nothing to do, carried her to the Jumping-Off Place."

III.

THE JUMPING-OFF PLACE.

THE children looked at Mr. Thimblefinger to see whether he was joking about the Jumping-Off Place, but he seemed to be very serious.

"I have heard of the Jumping-Off Place," remarked Mrs. Meadows, "but I had an idea it was just a saying."

"Well," replied Mr. Thimblefinger, "where you see a good deal of smoke, there must be some fire. When you hear a great many different people talking about anything, there must be something in it."

"What did the little girl see when she got to the Jumping-Off Place?" inquired Sweetest Susan.

"It was this way," said Mr. Thimblefinger: "When the whirlwinds from the south and the winds from the west, working in double harness, carried the thick clouds away, and the Thunder with them, the little girl went back to the place where she had left the old man who had carried her up the mountain.

"She found him waiting. He was sitting at the foot of a tree, sleeping peacefully, but he awoke at once.

"'You see I am waiting for you,' he said. 'How did you enjoy your visit?'

"'I did n't enjoy it much,' replied the little girl. 'Everything was so large, and the Thunder made so much fuss.'

"'I hope you did n't mind that,' said the old man. 'The Thunder is a great growler and grumbler, but when that 's said, all 's said. I am sorry, though, you did n't have a good time. I suppose you think it is my fault, but it is n't. If you say so, I 'll go to the Jumping-Off Place.'

"'Where is that?' asked the little girl.

"'Just beyond the Well at the End of the World.'

"'If it is n't too far, let 's go there,' said the little girl.

"So the old man lifted her on his back, and they went on their way. They must have gone very swiftly, for it was n't long before they came to the Well at the End of the World. An old woman was sitting near the Well, combing her hair. She paid no attention to the travelers, nor they to her. When they had gone beyond the Well a little distance, the little girl noticed that the sky appeared to be very close at hand. It was no longer blue, but dark, and seemed to hang down like a blanket or a curtain."

"But that could n't be, you know," said Buster John, "for the sky is no sky at all. It is nothing but space."

"How comes it dey call it sky, ef 't ain't no sky?" asked Drusilla, indignantly. "An' how come 't ain't no sky, when it 's right up dar, plain ez de han' fo' yo' face? Dat what I 'd like ter know."

"Why, the moon is thousands of miles away," said Buster John, "and some of the stars are millions and millions of miles farther than the moon."

"Dat what dey say," replied Drusilla, "but how dey know? Whar de string what dey medjud 'em wid? Tell me dat!"

"What about our sky?" asked Mrs. Meadows, smiling. "You would never think it was only the bottom of the spring if you did n't know it; now would you?"

Buster John had nothing to say in reply to this. Whereupon Sweetest Susan begged Mr. Thimblefinger to please go on with his story.

"Well," said he, "if I am to go on with it, I 'll have to tell it just as I heard it. I 'll have to put the sky just where I was told it was. When the little girl and the old man came close to the Jumping-Off Place, they saw that the sky was hanging close at hand. It may have been far, it may have been near, but to the little girl it seemed to be close enough to touch, and she wished very much for a long pole, so that she could see whether it was made of muslin or ging hams.

"Presently they came to a precipice. There was nothing beyond it and nothing below it. 'This,' said the old man to the little girl, 'is the Jumping-Off Place.'

"'Does any one jump off here?' said the little girl.

"'Not that I know of,' replied the old man, 'but if they should take a notion to, the place is all ready for them.'

"'Where would I fall to, if I jumped off?' the little girl asked.

" ' To Nowhere,' answered the old man.

" ' That is very funny,' said the little girl.

" ' Yes,' remarked the old man, ' you can get to the End of the World, but you would have to travel many a long year before you get to Nowhere. Some say it is a big city, some say it is a high mountain, and some say it is a wide plain.'

" The little girl went to the Jumping-Off Place and looked over, the old man holding her hand.

" ' Why, I see the moon shining down there,' she said. She was glad to see so familiar a face.

" The old man laughed. ' Yes,' he said, ' the moon is very fond of shining down there, and it runs away from the sun every chance it gets, and hunts up the darkest places, so that it may shine there undisturbed. To-day it is shining down there where the sun can't see it, but to-night it will creep up here, when the sun goes away, and shine the whole night through.'

" Turning back, the old man and the little girl came again to the Well at the End of the World. The old woman was sitting there, combing her long white hair. This time she looked hard at the little girl and smiled, singing : —

PRESENTLY THEY CAME TO A PRECIPICE

"'When the heart is young the well is dry —
Oh, it 's good-by, dearie! good-by!'

" But the old man shook his head. 'We have not come here for nothing, Sister Jane,' he said. With that he took a small vial, tied a long string to it, and let it down the well. He fished about until the vial was full of water, drew it to the top, and corked it tightly. The water sparkled in the sun as if it were full of small diamonds. Then he placed it carefully in his pocket, bowed politely to the old woman, who was still combing her long, white hair, and, smiling, lifted the little girl to his back, and returned along the road they had come, past the Thunder's house and down the mountain side, until they reached the little girl's home. Then he took the vial of sparkling water from his pocket. 'Take it,' he said, 'and wherever you go keep it with you. Touch a drop of it to your forehead when Friday is the thirteenth day of a month, and you will grow up to be both wise and beautiful. When you are in trouble, turn the vial upside down — so — and hold it in that position while you count twenty-six, and some of your friends will come to your aid.'

"The little girl thanked the old man as politely as she knew how.

"'Do you know why I have carried you to the Thunder's house and to the Jumping-Off Place, and why I have given you a vial of this rare water?' The little girl shook her head. 'Well, one day, not long ago, you were sitting by the roadside with some of your companions. You were all eating cake. A beggar came along and asked for a piece. You alone gave him any, and you gave him all you had.'

"'Were you the beggar?' asked the little girl, smiling and blushing.

"'That I leave you to guess,' replied the old man. He kissed the little girl's hand, and was soon hid from sight by a turn in the road."

Mr. Thimblefinger stopped short here, and waited to see what the children would say. They had listened attentively, but they manifested no very great interest.

"I reckon they think there is more talk than tale in what you have told," remarked Mr. Rabbit, leaning back in his chair. "That's the way it appeared to me."

"Well, I'll not say that I have come to the

end of my story," remarked Mr. Thimblefinger,
with some show of dignity, " but I have come to
the part where we can rest awhile, so as to give
Mr. Rabbit a chance to see if he can do any better. We 'll allow the little girl to grow some,
just as she does in the story."

IV.

"I 'm not much of a story-teller," said Mr. Rabbit, "and I never set up for one, but I will say that I like the rough-and-tumble tales a great deal better than I do the kind where some great somebody is always coming in with conjurings and other carryings-on. It 's on account of my raising, I reckon."

"Well, stories can't be all alike," remarked Mrs. Meadows. "You might as well expect a fiddle to play one tune."

"Tell us the kind of story you like best," said Buster John to Mr. Rabbit.

"No, not now," responded Mr. Rabbit. "I 'll do that some other time. I happened to think just now of a little circumstance that I used to hear mentioned when I was younger.

"In the country next door there used to be a great many chickens. Some were of the barn-yard breed, some were of the kind they call game, some were black, some were white, some were brown, some were speckled, and some had their feathers curled the wrong way. Among all these there was one whose name, as well as I can remember, was Mrs. Blue Hen."

"Was she really blue?" Sweetest Susan inquired.

"Well, not an indigo blue," replied Mr. Rabbit, after reflecting a moment, "nor yet a sky blue. She was just a plain, dull, every-day blue. But, such as she was, she was very fine. She belonged to one of the first families and moved in the very best circles. She was trim-looking, so I 've heard said, and, as she grew older, came to have a very bad temper, so much so that she used to fly at a hawk if he came near her premises. Some of her neighbors used to whisper it around that she tried to crow like a rooster, but this was after she had grown old and hard-headed.

"When Mrs. Blue Hen was growing up, she was very nice and particular. She could n't bear to get water on her feet, and she was always shaking the dust from her clothes. Some said she was finicky, and some said she was nervous. Once, when she fanned out little Billy Bantam,

who called on her one day, a great many of her
acquaintances said she would never settle down
and make a good housekeeper.

"But after awhile Mrs. Blue Hen concluded
that it was about time for her to have a family of
her own, so she went away off from the other
chickens and made her a nest in the middle of a
thick briar patch. She made her a nest there and
laid an egg. It was new and white, and Mrs.
Blue Hen was very proud of it. She was so
proud, in fact, that, although she had made up
her mind to make no fuss over it, she went running and cackling toward the house, just as any
common hen would do. She made so much fuss
that away down in the branch Mr. Willy Weasel
winked at Miss Mimy Mink.

" 'Do you hear that?' says he.

" 'I never heard anything plainer in my life,'
says she.

"Mrs. Blue Hen was so proud of her new,
white egg that she went back after awhile to look
at it. There it was, shining white in the grass.
She covered it up and hid it as well as she could,
and then she went about getting dinner ready.

"The next morning she went to the nest and

laid another egg just like the first one. This happened for three mornings; but on the fourth morning, when Mrs. Blue Hen went back, she found four eggs in the nest, and all four appeared to be dingy and muddy looking. She was very much astonished and alarmed, as well she might be, for here right before her eyes she saw four eggs, when she knew in reason that there should be but three; and not only that, they were all dingy and dirty.

"Mrs. Blue Hen was so excited that she took off her bonnet and began to fan herself. Then she wondered whether she had not made a miscount; whether she had not really laid four instead of three eggs. The more she thought about it, the more confused she became. She hung her bonnet on a blackberry bush and tried to count off the days on her toes. She began to count, — 'One, two, three,' — and she would have stopped there, but she could n't. She had four toes on her foot, and she was compelled to count them all. There was a toe on the foot for every egg in the nest.

"This caused Mrs. Blue Hen to feel somewhat more comfortable in mind and body, but she was

left in such a hysterical state that she went off
cackling nervously, and postponed laying an egg
until late in the afternoon.   After that there were
five in the nest, and she kept on laying until there
were ten altogether.   Then Mrs. Blue Hen rumpled up her feathers and got mad with herself, and
went to setting.   I reckon that 's what you call
it.   I 've heard some call it ' setting ' and others
' sitting.'   Once, when I was courting, I spoke of
a sitting hen, but the young lady said I was too
prissy for anything."

"What is prissy?" asked Sweetest Susan.

Mr. Rabbit shut his eyes and scratched his ear.
Then he shook his head slowly.

"It 's nothing but a girl's word," remarked
Mrs. Meadows by way of explanation.   "It means
that somebody 's trying hard to show off."

"I reckon that 's so," said Mr. Rabbit, opening his eyes.   He appeared to be much relieved.
"Well, Mrs. Blue Hen got mad and went to setting.   She was in a snug place and nobody bothered her.   It was such a quiet place that she could
hear Mr. Willy Weasel and Miss Mimy Mink gos-
siping in the calamus bushes, and she could hear
Mrs. Puddle Duck wading in the branch.   One

day Mrs. Puddle Duck made so bold as to push her way through the briars and look in upon Mrs. Blue Hen. But her visit was not relished. Mrs. Blue Hen rumpled her feathers up and spread out her tail to such a degree and squalled out such a harsh protest that Mrs. Puddle Duck was glad to waddle off with whole bones. But when she got back to the branch she spluttered about a good deal, crying out:

" ' Aha! aha! quack, quack! Aha! You are there, are you? Aha! you 'll have trouble before you get away. Aha!'

." Now the fact was that Mrs. Puddle Duck was the very one that had caused Mrs. Blue Hen all the trouble," said Mr. Rabbit, nodding his head solemnly. " While wading in the branch, Mrs. Puddle Duck had seen Mrs. Blue Hen going to her nest for three days, slipping and creeping through the weeds and bushes, and she wanted to know what all the slipping and creeping was about. So, on the third day Mrs. Puddle Duck did some slipping and creeping on her own account. She crept up close enough to see Mrs. Blue Hen on her nest, and she was near enough to see Mrs. Blue Hen when she ran away cackling.

"Then Mrs. Puddle Duck waddled up and peeped in the nest. There she saw three eggs as white and as smooth as ivory, and the sight filled her with jealousy. She began to talk to herself : —

"'I knew she must be mighty proud, the stuck-up thing! I can see that by the way she steps around here. Quack, quack! and I 'll just show her a thing or two.'

"Then and there Mrs. Puddle Duck, all muddy as she was, got in Mrs. Blue Hen's nest and sat on her beautiful white eggs and soiled them. And even that was not all. Out of pure spite Mrs. Puddle Duck laid one of her own dingy-looking eggs in Mrs. Blue Hen's nest, and that was the cause of all the trouble. That was the reason Mrs. Blue Hen found four dingy eggs in her nest when there ought to have been three clean white ones.

"Well, Mrs. Blue Hen went to setting, and after so long a time nine little chickens were hatched. She was very proud of them. She taught them how to talk, and then she wanted to get off her nest and teach them how to scratch about and earn their own living. But there was

ONE OF THEM WAS ENTIRELY DIFFERENT FROM ALL THE
REST

still one egg to hatch, and so Mrs. Blue Hen continued to set on it. One day she made up her mind to take her chicks off and leave the egg that would n't hatch. The old Speckled Hen happened to be passing and Mrs. Blue Hen asked her advice. But the old Speckled Hen was very much shocked when she heard the particulars.

" ' What! with nine chickens! ' she cried. ' Why, nine is an odd number. It would never do in the world. Hatch out the other egg.'

" But young people are very impatient, and Mrs. Blue Hen was young. She fretted and worried a good deal, but in a few days the tenth egg hatched. Mrs. Blue Hen felt very much better after this. In fact, she felt so comfortable that she did n't take the trouble to look at the chicken that hatched from the tenth egg. But when she brought her children off the nest she was very much astonished to find that one of them was entirely different from all the rest. She was not only surprised, but shocked. Nine of her children were as neat-looking as she could wish them to be, but the tenth one was a sight to see. It had weak eyes, a bill as broad as a case-knife, and big, flat feet. Its feet were so big that it waddled when it walked, and all the toes of each foot were joined together.

"Mrs. Blue Hen had very high notions. She wanted everybody to think that she belonged to the quality, but this wabbly chicken with a broad bill and a foot that had no instep to it took her pride down a peg. She kept her children hid as long as she could, but she had to come out in public after a while, and when she did — well, I 'll let you know there was an uproar in the barnyard. The old Speckled Hen was the first to begin it. She cried out: —

"'Look — look — look! Look at the Blue Hen's chickens!'

"Then the Guinea hens began to laugh, and the old Turkey Gobbler was so tickled he came near swallowing his snout. Mrs. Blue Hen hung her head with shame, and carried her children away off in the woods.

"But her flat-footed chicken gave rise to a by-word in all that country. When any stranger came along looking rough and ragged, it was the common saying that he was the Blue Hen's chicken."

"I 've heard it many a time," remarked Mrs. Meadows.

"There was no story in that," Buster John suggested.

"No," replied Mr. Rabbit. "Just some every-day facts picked up and strung together."

"Speaking of stories," said Mrs. Meadows, "I have one in my mind that is a sure enough story —one of the old-fashioned kind."

"Well, please, ma'am, tell it," said Buster John, so seriously that they all laughed except Mr. Rabbit.

V.

HOW A KING WAS FOUND.

"What about the little girl who had the vial of sparkling water?" said Sweetest Susan, turning to Mr. Thimblefinger, just as Mrs. Meadows was about to begin her story.

"Oh, she is growing," replied Mr. Thimblefinger.

Buster John frowned at his sister, as boys will do when they are impatient, and Sweetest Susan said no more.

"Once upon a time," Mrs. Meadows began, rubbing her chin thoughtfully, "there was a country that suddenly found itself without a king. This was a long time ago, before people in some parts of the world began to think it was unfashionable to have kings. I don't know what the trouble was exactly, whether the king died, or whether he was carried off, or whether he did something to cause the people to take away his crown and put him in the calaboose.

" Anyhow, they suddenly found themselves without a king, and it made them feel very uncomfortable. They were so restless and uneasy that they could n't sleep well at night. They were in the habit of having a king to govern them, and they felt very nervous without one.

" Now in that country there were eleven wise men whose trade it was to give advice. Instead of falling out and wrangling with one another and ruining their business, these eleven wise men had formed a copartnership and set up a sort of store, where anybody and everybody could get advice by the wholesale or retail. I don't know whether they charged anything, because there never has been a time since the world had more than two people in it that advice was n't as cheap as dirt.

" The eleven wise men were there, ready to give advice, and so the people went to them and asked them how to select a king. The eleven wise men put their heads together, and after a while they told the people that they must select nine of their best men and send them out on the roads leading to the capital city, and when these nine men found a man sleeping in the shade of a tree, they were to watch him for four hours, and if the shadow of the tree stood still so as to keep the sun from shining on him, he was the one to select for their king. Then the eleven wise men, looking very solemn, bowed the people out, and the people went off and selected nine of their best men to find them a king.

" Now it happened that in a part of the country not far from the capital city there lived a boy with his mother and stepfather. They were not poor and they were not rich, but everybody said the boy was the handsomest and brightest that had ever been seen in that section. He was about sixteen years old, and was very strong and tall.

" One day, when the stepfather was in the village near which they lived, a stranger passed through on his way to the capital city. He had neither wallet nor staff, but he drew a great crowd of idle people around him. He was carrying a red rooster, and although the fowl's feet were tied together and his head hanging down, he crowed lustily every few minutes. It was this that drew the crowd of idle people. One with more curiosity than the rest asked the stranger why the rooster crowed and continued to crow.

" 'He is a royal bird,' the stranger replied. 'There is no king in this country, and whoever eats this bird's head will reign as king.'

" 'He must be worth a pretty sum,' said one.

" 'By no means,' answered the stranger. 'He is worth no more than a silver piece.'

"But the people only laughed. They thought the stranger was making fun of them. He went on his way, and had soon passed beyond the village. Now it chanced that the stepfather of the bright and handsome boy was in the crowd that gathered around the stranger. He thought it was very queer that a rooster should be crowing so bravely when his legs were tied together and while his head was hanging down. So he said to himself that there might be some truth in what the stranger said. He ran after the man and soon overtook him.

" 'That is a fine fowl,' said the boy's stepfather.

" 'It is a royal bird,' the stranger replied.

" 'What is he worth?' asked the boy's stepfather.

" 'I shall be glad to get rid of him,' said the stranger. 'Give me a piece of silver and take him.'

"This was soon done, and the stepfather took the rooster under his arm.

"'Remember this,' remarked the stranger; 'if you eat the head of that bird you will reign in this country as king.'

"'Oh, ho!' laughed the boy's stepfather, 'you are a fine joker.'

"With the fowl under his arm he went toward his home. He had gone but a little way when he turned to look at the stranger, but the man had disappeared. The country was level for a long distance in all directions, but the stranger could not be seen.

"The boy's stepfather carried the fowl home and said to his wife : —

"'Cook this bird for supper. Cook the head also.'

"The man was afraid to tell his wife why he wanted the head cooked. He knew she was very fond of her son, and he reasoned to himself that if she knew what the stranger had said she would give the head to the boy. So he only told her to be careful to cook the fowl's head and save it for him.

"The wife did as she was bid. She cooked the

fowl and the fowl's head, and placed them away in the cupboard until her husband and her son came home. It happened that something kept the husband in the village a little later than usual, and while the woman was waiting for him her son came in and said he was very hungry.

"'You will find something in the cupboard,' his mother said. 'Eat a little now, and when your stepfather returns we will have supper.'

"The boy went to the cupboard. The fowl was on a big dish ready to be carved, and the head was in the saucer by itself. To save time and trouble the boy took the head and ate it, and then felt as if he could wait for supper very comfortably. The husband came, and the woman proceeded to set the table. When she came to look for the fowl's head it was gone.

"'Why, I ate it,' said her son, when he heard her exclamation of surprise. 'I found it in the saucer, and I ate it rather than cut the fowl.'

"The stepfather was angry enough to tear his hair, but he said nothing. The next day the boy went hunting. He was ready to return about noon, but, being tired, he stretched himself in the shade of a tree and was soon sound asleep.

" While he was sleeping his soundest, the nine men who had been appointed by the people to find them a king chanced to pass that way. They saw the handsome boy sleeping in the shade of the tree, and they stationed themselves around and watched him. For four long hours they watched the boy, but still the shadow of the tree kept the sun from his face. The nine men consulted among themselves, and they came to the conclusion that the shadow of the tree had n't moved, and that the boy was a well-favored lad who would look very well when he was dressed up and put on a throne with a crown on his head.

" So they shook the boy and aroused him from his sleep.

" ' What 's your name ? ' asked the spokesman.

" ' Telambus,' replied the boy.

" ' Where do you live ? '

" ' Not far from here.'

" ' How would you like to be king ? '

" ' I have never tried it. Is it an easy trade to learn ? '

" The nine men looked at each other shrewdly and smiled. They each had the same thought.

" They went with the boy to his home and saw

THEY SAW THE HANDSOME BOY SLEEPING

his mother, and inquired about his age and his education, and asked a hundred other questions besides. They cautioned the woman as they were leaving to say nothing of their visit except this, that they were going about hunting for a king and had called to make some inquiries.

" When her husband came home he had already heard of the visit of the distinguished company, and so he asked his wife a thousand questions. All the answer he got was that the visitors were hunting for a king.

" 'I 'm sure it was for me they were hunting,' said the man. 'How unfortunate that I was away.'

" 'Well, don't worry,' replied his wife. 'If they ever intended to make you king, they 'll come back after you.'

" 'You don't seem to think much about it,' remarked the man, 'but some of these days you 'll find out that you narrowly escaped being the king's wife.'

" The nine citizens were so certain that they had found the right person to rule over their country as king, that they made haste to return to the capital city and tell the news to the eleven wise men who had sent them out. They made their report, and the eleven wise men put their heads together once more. When they had consulted together a long time, they said to the people : —

" 'There is one test by which you may know whether a king has been found. Send a messenger and ask this young man to send us a rope made of sand a hundred feet long.'

" The messenger straightway went to the house of Telambus and told him what the eleven wise men had said. His mother straightway fell to crying. But Telambus laughed at her fears.

" 'Tell the eleven wise men,' he said to the messenger, 'that there are various patterns of sand ropes. Let them send me a sample of the kind they want — a piece only a foot long — and I will make them one a hundred feet long.'

" The messenger returned to the eleven wise men and told them what Telambus had said. They put their heads together again and then told the people that the young man was wise enough to be their king. There was great rejoicing then, and the nine wise men who had found him went to fetch him.

"But Telambus shook his head. 'Kings are not carried about in this way. Where are your banners and your chariots? Where are your drums and your cymbals?'

"So the nine men returned to the eleven wise men and told them what Telambus had said.

"'He is right,' said the eleven wise men. 'He is a king already. Get your horses, your chariots, your banners, and your music, and bring our king in as he deserves to be brought.'

"So Telambus was made the king of that country."

At this point Mrs. Meadows began to hunt for a knitting-needle she had dropped, and the children knew that the story was ended.

"That was a pretty good story," said Mr. Thimblefinger. "It was short and sweet, as the king-bird said to the honey-bee."

"Dey wuz too much kingin' in it ter suit me. Ef folks got ter have kings, how come we ain't got none?" asked Drusilla.

"Please tell me about the little girl with the vial of sparkling water from the Well at the End of the World," said Sweetest Susan to Mr. Thimblefinger. "I expect she is nearly grown by this time."

"Oh, yes," replied Mr. Thimblefinger, "she has now grown to be quite a young lady."

"Huh!" grunted Drusilla, "ef folks grow up dat quick, I dunner what hinder me from bein' a ol' gray-head 'oman by sundown."

VI.

" DON'T you see," said Mr. Thimblefinger, with apparent seriousness, "that if we had n't left off the story of the little girl who went to the Well at the End of the World just where we did, she would have had no time to grow?"

Buster John smiled faintly, but Sweetest Susan took the statement seriously, though she said nothing. Drusilla boldly indorsed it.

"I speck dat 's so," she said, "kaze when de lil' gal got back home wid dat vial she wa'n't in no fix fer ter cut up dem kind er capers what de tales tell about."

"Certainly not," remarked Mr. Thimblefinger, "but now she has had time to grow up to be a young lady, almost. Names go for so little down here that I have n't told you hers. She was named Eolen. Some said it was a beautiful name, but her stepmother and her stepmother's daughter said it was very ugly. Anyhow, that was her name, and whether it was ugly or whether it was beautiful, she had to make the best of it.

" Well, Eolen went home when the old man gave her the vial of water from the Well at the End of the World. She hid the vial beneath her apron until she reached her own room, and then she placed it at the very bottom of her little trunk, — a trunk that had belonged to her mother, who was dead.

" Nothing happened for a long time. Whenever Friday fell on the thirteenth of a month, Eolen would rub a drop of the sparkling water on her forehead, and she grew to be the loveliest young lady that ever was seen. Her stepsister was not bad-looking, but, compared with Eolen, she was ugly. The contrast between them was so great that people could not help noticing it and making remarks about it. Some of these remarks came to the ears of her stepmother.

" Now a stepmother can be just as nice and as good as anybody, but this particular stepmother cared for nothing except her own child, and she soon came to hate Eolen for being so beautiful. She had never treated the child kindly, but now she began to treat her cruelly. Eolen never told her father, but somehow he seemed to know what was going on, and he treated her more affectionately each day, as her stepmother grew more cruel.

"This lasted for some time, but finally Eolen's father fell ill and died, and then, although she had many admirers, she was left without a friend she could confide in or rely on. To make matters worse, her stepmother produced a will in which her husband had left everything to her and nothing to Eolen. The poor girl did n't know what to do. She knew that her father had made no such will, but how could she prove it? She happened to think of the vial of sparkling waters. She found it and turned it upside down.

" On the instant there was a loud knock at the street door. Eolen would have gone to open it, but her stepmother was there before her. She peeped from behind the curtains in the hallway, and saw a tall, richly-dressed stranger standing on the steps.

"'I wish to see a young lady who lives here. She is the daughter of an old friend,' said the stranger.

" The stepmother smiled very sweetly. 'Come in. I will call her.'

"But instead of calling Eolen she called her own daughter. The girl went, but not with a good grace. She had been petted and spoiled, and was very saucy and impolite. The stranger smiled when he saw her.

"'What was my mother doing when you saw her sitting by the Well at the End of the World?' he asked.

"'Do you take me for a crazy person?' replied the girl.

"'By no means,' said the stranger. 'You are not the young lady I came to see.'

"The stepmother then called Eolen and stood in the room frowning to see what was going to happen. Eolen came as soon as she was called, and the stranger seemed to be much struck by her beauty and modesty. He took her by the hand and led her to a chair.

"'What was my mother doing when you saw her sitting by the Well at the End of the World?' he asked.

"'She was combing her hair,' replied Eolen.

"'That is true,' remarked the stranger. 'Yes, she was combing her hair.' Then he turned to the stepmother and said: 'May I see this young

lady alone for a little while? I have a message
for her from an old friend.'

" 'Certainly!' the stepmother answered. 'I
hope her friend is well-to-do, for her father has
died without leaving her so much as a farthing.'
Having said this, the stepmother flounced from
the room.

" 'I came at your summons,' said the stranger;
'you turned the vial of sparkling water upside
down, and now I am here to do your bidding.'

" Then Eolen told him of the death of her
father, and how he had left all of his property
to her stepmother. The stranger listened attentively, and while he listened played with a heavy
gold ring that he wore on his third finger. When
Eolen was through with her story he took this
ring from his finger and handed it to her.

" 'Look through that,' he said, 'and tell me
what you see.'

" Eolen held the ring to one of her eyes, and
peeped through the golden circle. She was so
surprised that she came near dropping the ring.
She had held it up toward the stranger, but instead of seeing him through the ring she seemed
to be looking into a room in which some person

was moving about. As she continued to look, the scene appeared to be a familiar one. The room was the one her stepmother occupied — the room in which her father had died. She saw her stepmother take from her father's private drawer a folded paper and hide it behind the mantel. Then the scene vanished, and through the ring she saw the stranger smiling at her.

" ' What you have seen happened some time ago.' He took the ring and replaced it on his finger. ' Your stepmother is now coming this way. She has been trying to hear what we are saying. When she comes in, do you get your father's real will from behind the mantel and bring it to me.'

" Sure enough the stepmother came into the room silently and suddenly. She pretended to be much surprised to find any one there.

" ' You must excuse me,' she said to the stranger. ' I imagined I heard you take your leave some time ago.'

" ' You are excusable,' replied the stranger. ' I have been reflecting rather than talking. I have been thinking what could be done for your stepdaughter, who must be quite a burden to you.'

"The stepmother took this for an invitation to tell what she knew about Eolen, and you may be sure she did n't waste any praise on the young lady. But right in the midst of it all Eolen, who had gone out, returned and handed the stranger the folded paper that had been hid behind the mantel. The stepmother recognized it and turned pale.

" 'This,' said the stranger, opening the paper and reading it at a glance, 'is your father's will. I see he has left you half the property.'

" 'That is the will my husband forgot to destroy,' cried the stepmother. 'I have the real will.'

" 'May I see it?' asked the stranger.

"The stepmother ran to fetch it, but when the stranger had opened it, not a line nor a word of writing could be found on it.

" 'I see you are fond of a joke,' said the stranger, but the stepmother had fallen into a chair and sat with her face hid in her hands. 'I am fond of a joke myself,' continued the stranger, 'and I think I can match yours.'

"With that the stranger took the real will, tore it in small pieces and threw it into the fireplace.

" ' What have you done?' cried Eolen.

" ' The most difficult thing in the world,' replied the stranger; ' I have made this lady happy.'

" And sure enough the stepmother was smiling and thanking him.

" ' I thought you were my enemy,' she said, ' but now I see you are my friend indeed. How can I repay you?'

" ' By treating this young lady here as your daughter,' he replied. ' Have no fear,' he said, turning to Eolen. ' No harm can befall you. What I have done is for the best.'

" But before he went away he gave Eolen the gold ring, and told her to wear it for the sake of his mother, who sat by the Well at the End of the World. She thanked him for his kindness and promised she would keep the ring and treasure it as long as she lived.

" But there was one trouble with this magic ring. It was too large for any of Eolen's fingers. She had the whitest and most beautiful hands ever seen, but the ring would fit none of her fingers. Around her neck she wore a necklace of coral beads, and on this necklace she hung the ring.

"For many days Eolen's stepmother was kind to her, almost too kind. But the woman was afraid her stepdaughter would inform the judges of her effort to steal and hide her husband's will. The judges were very severe in those days and in that country, and if the woman had been brought before them and such a crime proven on her, she would have been sent to the rack."

"What is a rack?" asked Sweetest Susan.

"Hit 's de place whar dey scrunch folks's ve'y vitals out'n 'em," said Drusilla solemnly.

"That 's about right, I reckon," assented Mr. Thimblefinger. "Well, the stepmother was as kind to Eolen as she knew how to be, but the kindness did n't last long. She hated her stepdaughter worse than ever. She was afraid of her, but she did n't hate her any the less on that account.

"Eolen had a habit of taking off her coral necklace and placing it under her pillow at night. One night, when she was fast asleep, her stepmother crept into the room and slipped the ring from the necklace. She had no idea it was a magic ring. She said to herself that it would look better on her daughter's finger than it did on Eolen's coral necklace, so she took the ring and slipped it on the finger of her sleeping daughter, and then stepped back a little to admire the big golden circle on the coarse, red hand.

"Almost immediately the daughter began to toss and tumble in her sleep. She flung her arms wildly about and tried to talk. The mother, becoming alarmed, tried to wake her, but it was some time before the girl could be roused from her troubled sleep.

"'Oh!' she cried, when she awoke, 'what is the matter with me? I dreamed some one was cutting my finger off. What was it? Oh! it hurts me still!'

"She held up the finger on which her mother had placed the ring and tried to tear off the golden band. 'It burns — it burns!' she cried. 'Take it off.'

"Her mother tried to take the ring off, but it was some time before she succeeded. Her daughter struggled and cried so that it was a hard matter to remove the ring, which seemed to be as hot as fire. A red blister was left on the girl's finger, and she was in great pain.

"'What have I done?' the mother cried, see-

HER STEPMOTHER CREPT INTO THE ROOM

ing her daughter's condition. The two made so much noise that Eolen awoke and went to the door to find out what the trouble was.

" 'Go away, you hussy!' screamed the step-mother when she saw Eolen at the door. 'Go away! You are a witch!'

" 'Why, what have I done?' Eolen asked.

" 'You are the cause of all this trouble. For amusement I placed your gold ring on my dear daughter's finger, and now see her condition!'

" 'Why, then, did you take my ring? If you had left it where I placed it, you would have had none of this trouble.' Eolen spoke with so much dignity that her stepmother was surprised into silence, though she could talk faster and louder than a flutter-mill. But finally she found her voice.

" 'Go away! You are a witch!' she said to Eolen.

"But Eolen went boldly into the room. 'Give me my ring!' she exclaimed. 'You shall wrong me no further. Give me my ring! I will have it!'

"This roused the stepmother's temper. She searched on the floor till she found the ring.

Then she opened a window and flung it as far as she could send it.

" ' Now let 's see you get it ! ' she cried. With that she seized Eolen by the arm and pushed her from the room, saying, ' Go away, you witch ! '

" Now, then," said Mr. Thimblefinger, after pausing to take breath, " what was the poor girl to do ? " He looked at Sweetest Susan as if expecting her to answer the question.

" I 'm sure I don't know," replied Sweetest Susan.

" Shake up de bottle," exclaimed Drusilla.

" Exactly so," said Mr. Thimblefinger.

VII.

"I HOPE that is n't all of the story, — if you call it a story," said Buster John.

"Which?" remarked Mr. Thimblefinger, with an air of having forgotten the whole business.

"Why, that about throwing the gold ring from the window," replied Buster John.

"Well, no," said Mr. Thimblefinger, in an absent-minded way. "In a book, you know, you can read right on if you want to, or you can put the book down and rest yourself when you get tired. But when I 'm telling a story, you must give me time to rest. I 'm so little, you know, that it does n't take much to tire me. Of course, if you don't like the story, I can stop any time. It 's no trouble at all to stop. Just wink your eye at me twice, and I 'm mum."

"Oh, we don't want you to stop," said Sweetest Susan.

"No, don't stop," remarked Mr. Rabbit, drowsily, "because then everybody gets to talking, and I can't doze comfortably. Your stories are as comforting to me as a feather-bed."

"Then I 'll add a bolster to the bed," exclaimed Mr. Thimblefinger. He hesitated a moment, and then went on with the story: —

"Of course, Eolen did n't know what to do when her stepmother threw the gold ring from the window and pushed her from the room. She went back to her bed and lay down, but she could n't sleep. After a while daylight came, and then she dressed herself and went down into the garden to hunt for the ring. She searched everywhere, but the ring was not to be found.

"Now the ring could have been found very easily if it had been where it fell when Eolen's stepmother threw it from the window. But that night a tame crow, belonging to the Prince of that country, was roosting in one of the trees in the garden."

"Oh, was it a sure enough Prince?" asked Sweetest Susan.

"Why, certainly," replied Mr. Thimblefinger, with great solemnity. "A make-believe Prince could never have reigned in that country. The

people would have found him out, and he would
have been put in the calaboose. Well, this tame
crow that belonged to the Prince had wandered
off over the fields, and had gone so far away from
the palace that it was unable to get back before
dark, and so it went to bed in one of the trees
growing in the garden behind the house where
Eolen lived.

" Of course, as soon as morning came, the crow
was wide awake and ready for any mischief that
might turn up. It flew to the ground, hoping to
find something for breakfast, and hopped about,
searching in the leaves and grass. Suddenly the
crow saw the ring shining on the ground and
picked it up and turned it over. What could it
be? The crow's curiosity was such that it forgot
all about breakfast. It seized the ring in its beak
and went flopping to the palace. It was so early
in the morning that the palace was closed, but the
crow flew straight to the Prince's window and beat
his wings against it until some of the attendants
came and opened it, when the crow walked in
with great dignity.

" The Prince had been awakened by the noise,
but when he saw the bird stalking into the room

as stiff as a major-general of militia, he fell back on his bed laughing. The crow hopped to the foot-board of the bed and stood there holding the gold ring in his beak, as much as to say, 'Don't you wish you were as rich as I am?'

"The Prince rose from his bed and took the ring from the crow, but it was so hot that he made haste to drop it in a basin of cold water. Then a curious thing happened. The ring seemed to expand in the basin until it was as large as the bottom, and within the circle it made the picture of a beautiful girl standing by a milk-white cow. There were two peculiarities about the milk-white cow. Her ears were as black as jet, and her horns shone and glittered as if they were made of gold.

"The Prince was entranced. He gazed at the beautiful picture long and lovingly, and the crow sat on the rim of the basin and chuckled as proudly as if it had painted the picture. The girl was the loveliest the Prince had ever seen, and the cow was surely the most beautiful of her kind. The Prince's attendants uttered exclamations of delight when they saw the picture, and his ministers, when they were sent for, were struck dumb with astonishment.

" 'If this bird could only speak!' cried the Prince.

" But the crow went chuckling about the room saying to itself, ' What a fool a Prince must be who cannot understand my simple language!'

" The Prince gazed at the picture framed by the gold ring for a long time. At last he concluded to take it from the water. As he did so it shrunk to its natural size, and the picture of the beautiful girl and the Cow with the Golden Horns disappeared, and the ring no longer burnt his fingers. He dropped it in the basin once more, but it remained a simple gold ring and the picture failed to appear again.

" The Prince was disconsolate. He remained in the palace and refused to go out. He moped and pined, until the family doctor was called in. The doctor fussed about and felt of the Prince's pulse and looked at his tongue, and said that a change of air was necessary; but the Prince said he did n't want any change of air and would n't have it. In fact, he said he did n't want any air at all, and he would n't take any pills or powders, and he would n't drink any sage tea, and he would n't have any mustard plaster put on him.

He was in love, and he knew that the more medicine he took, the worse off he would be."

" Well, a little sage tea ain't bad when you are in love," remarked Mrs. Meadows. " It 's mighty soothing."

" Maybe," continued Mr. Thimblefinger, " but the Prince did n't want it, and would n't have it. He wanted the beautiful girl he had seen in the picture. He was in love with her, and he wanted to marry her. So his ministers consulted together and finally they sent around a bailiff " —

" Nonsense ! " cried Mrs. Meadows.

" Tut — tut ! " exclaimed Mr. Rabbit.

" Well," said Mr. Thimblefinger, " he sent a crier around " —

" A herald, you mean," suggested Buster John, who had read a good many story books.

" A bailiff could do the work just as well, but you can have it your way. Well," continued Mr. Thimblefinger, " the Prince's ministers sent a herald around to inquire at all the people's houses if any of them had a Cow with Golden Horns, but nobody had such a cow, and everybody wondered what the herald meant. A Cow with Golden Horns ! People went about asking one another if they had ever heard of such a thing before. Some said the throne was tottering. Others said the politicians were trying to work a scheme to increase taxation. Still others talked about the peril of the nation. Everybody had some explanation, but nobody had the right one. The poor young Prince was nearly crazy to find the young girl whose picture he had seen in the basin of water.

"For a few days the people heard no more of the matter, but at the end of a week the herald went round the city again declaring that the Prince would marry any young lady who would bring as her marriage portion a Cow with Golden Horns. She need not have riches of any kind; all that was necessary was a Cow with Golden Horns. This word went around among the people and from city to city. Rich men with daughters tried everywhere to buy a Cow with Golden Horns, but all to no purpose.

"The Prince waited and waited and pined and grew thinner. But just as matters were getting to be very serious indeed, an old man appeared in the palace park leading a beautiful white cow with jet black ears and golden horns. The ser-

vants set up such a shout when they saw the beautiful cow that everybody in the palace was aroused
and all came out to see what caused the noise.
Then the servants and attendants ran over one
another in their efforts to reach the Prince, who
was moping in his room. As they ran they
cried : —

"'The Cow with the Golden Horns has come!
The Cow with the Golden Horns has come!'

"The Prince forgot his dignity and hurried out
to see the Cow with the Golden Horns. The old
man came leading her, and she was, indeed, a
beautiful creature. Her head and limbs were almost as delicate as those of a deer, and her eyes
were large and soft. Her body was as white as
snow, her ears glistened like black silk, and her
golden horns shone in the sun. The old man
bowed low as he led the beautiful cow forward.

"'I would n't make much of a bride myself,
your Majesty,' he said. 'I have brought you the
Cow with the Golden Horns. She might find you
the bride that I failed to bring you.'

"'I fear I shall have no such good fortune,'
replied the Prince. 'But I think you have proved
to me that I am not dreaming. How shall I
reward you?'

" 'I ask no reward, your Majesty. I only ask the privilege of taking away my Cow with the Golden Horns when you have found your bride.'

" When the Prince had given his promise, the old man said, 'You have a ring, your Majesty, that came to you in a curious way. Let this ring be placed on the left horn of the cow. The girl or woman that is able to remove this ring will be the bride you are wishing for. Every morning the Cow with the Golden Horns will appear here in the lawn and remain until night falls. Let it be announced, your Majesty, that whoever takes the ring from her shall be the Princess of the Realm.' "

" Huh! " exclaimed Drusilla suddenly. " He talk like he been ter college."

" Will you hush? " cried Buster John. But Mr. Thimblefinger paid no attention to the interruption.

" 'But how do you know,' asked the Prince, 'that the right one will come to get the ring?'

" 'How do I know that your Majesty has the ring?' the old man answered.

" This seemed to satisfy the Prince, who caused it to be announced all through his kingdom that he would choose for his bride the girl or woman who would take the ring from the golden horn of the Cow.

"Of course there was a great commotion among the ladies when this announcement was made, and nearly all of them tried to take the ring from the golden horn of the Cow. Some said they tried it just for fun, and some said they tried it just out of curiosity; but all of them failed. Even Eolen's stepmother tried, and then she made her daughter try, but when the daughter touched the ring it burnt her so that she screamed. And then some of those who had tried and failed turned up their noses and said it was a trick.

"Eolen had never thought of trying. She had seen the Prince and admired him, yet she had no idea of going up before all these people. But as soon as her stepmother started for the palace with her daughter, there came a knock at the door. Eolen opened it, and there, standing before her, was the old man who had carried her to the Thunder's house, and to the Jumping-Off Place. She was very glad to see him, and told him so, and he was just as glad to see her.

"'Why don't you go and get your ring?' he asked.

" 'It is lost,' she answered.

" 'It is found,' he said. 'I have placed it on the golden horn of thé Cow that stands near the palace door. You must go and get it.'

" 'I have nothing to wear,' she replied.

" Then the old man tapped on the wall and called : —

" 'Sister Jane! Sister Jane! Where are you?'

" 'I am where I ought to be,' was the reply. The wall opened and out stepped the old, old woman that Eolen had seen combing her hair by the Well at the End of the World.

" 'Clothe this child in silk and satin and comb her hair out fine, Sister Jane.'

" The old woman grumbled a little, but gave Eolen a touch here and there, and in a moment she was dressed as fine as the finest lady in the land.

" 'Now she is ready, brother,' said the old, old woman, and then she disappeared in the wall, combing her long gray hair and smiling.

" 'Must I walk?' asked Eolen, looking at her satin slippers.

" 'Nonsense!' exclaimed the old man. Then

he tapped in another part of the wall.   'Nephew!
Nephew!   Where are you?'

"'Wherever you wish me to be,' a voice replied, and then the wall opened, and out stepped
the handsome stranger who had given Eolen the
gold ring.   'What do you want?'

"'A carriage and horses,' said the old man.

"'They are at the door,' was the reply, 'and
I'll drive them myself.'

"Sure enough, there stood at the door a coach
and four, and Eolen was carried to the palace
in grand style.   Liveried servants appeared and
spread a strip of carpet before her, and the Cow
with the Golden Horns came running to meet her,
and in a moment she had the ring.   Then the
people set up a loud shout, crying: —

"'The Princess! the Princess!'

"And then the Prince came out and went to
her.   She would have knelt, but he lifted her up
and knelt himself before her, and kissed her hand,
and smiled on her, for she was the lovely girl he
had seen in the picture."

"What is the moral of that?" inquired Mr.
Rabbit, waking from his nap.

"Why, you did n't even hear the story," said
Mr. Thimblefinger.

SHE WOULD HAVE KNELT, BUT HE LIFTED HER UP

"That is the reason I want to hear the moral of it," remarked Mr. Rabbit.

"There is no moral at all," said Mr. Thimble-finger.

"Then I'm mighty glad I was asleep," grumbled Mr. Rabbit.

VIII.

BROTHER WOLF'S TWO BIG DINNERS.

THE children said they were very much pleased with the story about the Cow with the Golden Horns. Buster John even went so far as to say that it was as good as some of the stories in the books. But Mr. Thimblefinger shook his head. He said he was very glad they were pleased with it, but he knew Mr. Rabbit was right. The story could n't be a very good story, because it had no moral.

"But I think it had a very good moral," remarked Mrs. Meadows.

"What was it?" inquired Mr. Rabbit with great solemnity.

"Why, if the little girl had been too stingy to give the old beggar a piece of her cake, she would never have come to be Princess," replied Mrs. Meadows.

"Did she give the beggar a piece of cake?" asked Mr. Rabbit.

"Why, certainly she did," Mr. Thimblefinger answered.

"Well," remarked Mr. Rabbit, setting himself back in his chair, "I must have been fast asleep when she did it. But the place for a moral, as I 've been told, is right at the end of a story, and not at the beginning."

"Can't you tell us a story with a moral?" suggested Mrs. Meadows.

"I can," replied Mr. Rabbit. "I can for a fact, and the piece of cake you mentioned puts me in mind of it."

Mr. Rabbit closed his eyes and rubbed his nose, and then began : —

"Once upon a time, when Brother Fox and myself were living on pretty good terms with each other, we received an invitation to attend a barbecue that Brother Wolf was going to give on the following Saturday. The next day we received an invitation to a barbecue that Brother Bear was going to give on the same Saturday.

"I made up my mind at once to go to Brother Bear's barbecue, because I knew he would have fresh roasting ears, and if there 's anything I like better than another, it is fresh roasting ears.

I asked Brother Fox whether he was going to Brother Bear's barbecue or to Brother Wolf's, but he shook his head. He said he had n't made up his mind. I just asked him out of idle curiosity, for I did n't care whether he went or whether he stayed.

"I went about my work as usual. Cold weather was coming on, and I wanted to get my crops in before the big freeze came. But I noticed that Brother Fox was mighty restless in his mind. He did n't do a stroke of work. He 'd sit down and then he 'd get up; he 'd stand still and look up in the tops of the trees, and then he 'd walk back and forth with his hands behind him and look down at the ground.

"I says to him, says I, 'I hope you are not sick, Brother Fox.'

"Says he, 'Oh, no, Brother Rabbit; I never felt better in my life.'

"I says to him, says I, 'I hope money matters are not troubling you.'

"Says he, 'Oh, no, Brother Rabbit, money was never easier with me than it is this season.'

"I says to him, says I, 'I hope I 'll have the pleasure of your company to the barbecue to-morrow.'

" Says he, ' I can't tell, Brother Rabbit; I can't tell. I have n't made up my mind. I may go to the one, or I may go to the other; but which it will be, I can't tell you to save my life.'

" As the next day was Saturday, I was up bright and early. I dug my goobers and spread 'em out to dry in the sun, and then, ten o'clock, as near as I could judge, I started out to the barbecue. Brother Wolf lived near the river, and Brother Bear lived right on the river, a mile or two below Brother Wolf's. The big road, that passed near where Brother Fox and I lived, led in the direction of the river for about three miles, and then it forked, one prong going to Brother Wolf's house, and the other prong going to Brother Bear's house.

" Well, when I came to the forks of the road, who should I see there but old Brother Fox. I stopped before he saw me, and watched him. He went a little way down one road, and licked his chops; then he came back and went a little way down the other road, and licked his chops.

" Not choosing to be late, I showed myself and passed the time of day with Brother Fox. I said, says I, that if he was going to Brother Bear's barbecue, I 'd be glad to have his company.   But he said, says he, that he would n't keep me waiting. He had just come down to the forks of the road to see if that would help him to make up his mind. I told him I was mighty sorry to miss his company and his conversation, and then I tipped my hat and took my cane from under my arm and went down the road that led to Brother Bear's house."

Here Mr. Rabbit paused, straightened himself up a little, and looked at the children.   Then he continued : —

" I reckon you all never stood on the top of a hill three quarters of a mile from the smoking pits and got a whiff or two of the barbecue ? "

" I is ! I is ! " exclaimed Drusilla.   " Don't talk ! Hit make me dribble at de mouf.   I wish I had some right now."

" Well," said Mr. Rabbit, " I got a whiff of it and I was truly glad I had come — truly glad.   It was a fine barbecue, too.   There was lamb, and kid, and shote, all cooked to a turn and well seasoned, and then there was the hash made out of the giblets.   I 'll not tell you any more about the dinner, except that I 'd like to have one like it

HE WENT A LITTLE WAY DOWN ONE ROAD

every Saturday in the year. If I happened to be too sick to eat it, I could sit up and look at it. Anyhow, we all had enough and to spare.

"After we had finished with the barbecue and were sitting in Brother Bear's front porch smoking our pipes and talking politics, I happened to mention to Brother Bear something about Brother Wolf's barbecue. I said, says I, that I thought I 'd go by Brother Wolf's house as I went on home, though it was a right smart step out of the way, just to see how the land lay.

"Says Brother Bear, says he : ' If you 'll wait till my company take their leave, I don't mind trotting over to Brother Wolf's with you. The walk will help to settle my dinner.'

"So, about two hours by sun, we started out and went to Brother Wolf's house. Brother Bear knew a short cut through the big canebrake, and it did n't take us more than half an hour to get there. Brother Wolf was just telling his company good-by; and when they had all gone he would have us go in and taste his mutton stew, and then he declared he 'd think right hard of us if we did n't drink a mug or two of his persimmon beer.

"I said, says I, 'Brother Wolf, have you seen Brother Fox to-day?'

"Brother Wolf said, says he, 'I declare, I have n't seen hair nor hide of Brother Fox. I don't see why he did n't come. He's always keen to go where there's fresh meat a-frying.'

"I said, says I, 'The reason I asked was because I left Brother Fox at the forks of the road trying to make up his mind whether he 'd eat at your house or at Brother Bear's.'

"'Well, I 'm mighty sorry,' says Brother Wolf, says he; 'Brother Fox never missed a finer chance to pick a bone than he 's had to-day. Please tell him so for me.'

"I said I would, and then I told Brother Wolf and Brother Bear good-by and set out for home. Brother Wolf's persimmon beer had a little age on it, and it made me light-headed and nimble-footed. I went in a gallop, as you may say, and came to the forks of the road before the sun went down.

"You may not believe it, but when I got there Brother Fox was there going through the same motions that made me laugh in the morning — running down one road and licking his chops, and then running down the other and licking his chops.

"Says I, 'I hope you had a good dinner at Brother Wolf's to-day, Brother Fox.'

"Says he, 'I 've had no dinner.'

"Says I, 'That 's mighty funny. Brother Bear had a famous barbecue, and I thought Brother Wolf was going to have one, too.'

"Says Brother Fox, 'Is dinner over? Is it too late to go?'

"Says I, 'Why, Brother Fox, the sun 's nearly down. By the time you get to Brother Bear's house, he 'll be gone to bed; and by the time you go across the swamp to Brother Wolf's house, the chickens will be crowing for day.'

"'Well, well, well!' says Brother Fox, 'I 've been all day trying to make up my mind which road I 'd take, and now it 's too late.'

"And that was the fact," continued Mr. Rabbit. "The poor creature had been all day trying to make up his mind which road he 'd take. Now, then, what is the moral?"

Sweetest Susan looked at Mrs. Meadows, but Mrs. Meadows merely smiled. Buster John rattled the marbles in his pocket.

"I know," said Drusilla.

"What?" inquired Mr. Rabbit.

"Go down one road an' git one dinner, den cut 'cross an' git some mo' dinner, an' den go back home down de yuther road."

Mr. Rabbit shook his head.

"Tar Baby, you are wrong," he said.

"If you want anything, go and get it," suggested Buster John.

Mr. Rabbit shook his head and looked at Sweetest Susan, whereupon she said: —

"If you can't make up your mind, you'll have to go hungry."

Mr. Rabbit shook his head.

"Eat a good breakfast," said Mrs. Meadows, "and you won't be worried about your dinner."

"All wrong!" exclaimed Mr. Rabbit, with a chuckle. "The moral is this: He who wants too much is more than likely to get nothing."

"Well," remarked Mrs. Meadows dubiously, "if you have to work out a moral as if it was a sum in arithmetic, I'll thank you not to trouble me with any more morals."

"The motion is seconded and carried," exclaimed Mr. Thimblefinger.

IX

THE LITTLE BOY OF THE LANTERN.

"Of course," said Mr. Thimblefinger, "all of you can tell better stories than I can, because you are larger. Being taller, you can see farther and talk louder; but I sometimes think that if I was to climb a tree, I 'd see as far as any of you."

"Well, I hope your feelings are not hurt," remarked Mr. Rabbit sympathetically. "It 's not the fault of your stories that I fall asleep when you are telling them. It 's my habit to sit and nod at certain hours of the day, and if you 'll watch me right close, you 'll see that I sometimes drop off when I 'm telling a story myself. I 'll try and keep awake the next time you tell one."

"I 'm afraid I 'll have to prop Mr. Rabbit's eyelids open with straws," said Mrs. Meadows, laughing.

"I 'll just try you with a little one," Mr. Thimblefinger declared. "I 'll tell you one I heard when I was younger. I want to see whether

Mr. Rabbit will keep awake, and I want to see whether there 's a moral in the tale."

So he took off his little hat, which was shaped like a thimble, and run his hand over the feather ornament to straighten it out. Then he began : —.

" A long time ago, when there was a great deal more room in the country next door than there is now, there lived a man who had a wife, one son, a horse, a cow, and a calf. He was a hard-working man, so much so that he had little or no time to devote to his family. He worked hard in the field all day, and when night came he was too tired to trouble much about his son. His wife, too, having no servant, was always busy about the house, sewing, washing, cooking, cleaning, patching, milking, and sweeping. Day in and day out it was always the same. The man was always working, and the woman was always working. They had no rest except on Sunday, and then they were too tired to pay much attention to their son.

" The consequence was, that while the boy was a very bright lad, he was full of mischief, up to all sorts of tricks and pranks that some people call meanness. By hook or by crook — or maybe by book — he had learned how to spell and read. But the only book he had to read was one with big pictures of men dressed in red clothes, and armed with yellow cutlasses. The book was called 'The Pirooters of Peruvia.'"

"Maybe the name was 'The Pirates of Peru,'" suggested Buster John.

"Oh, no," replied Mr. Thimblefinger. "I don't suppose any such country as Peru had been found on the map when that book was written. But never mind about that. The boy read only that book, and he became rather wild in his mind. He wanted to be a pirooter, whatever that was, and so he armed himself with old hoe helves and called them pikes, and he tied a shingle to his side and called it a cutlass, and he got him a broom-handle and called it a horse.

"This boy's name was Johnny, but sometimes they called him Jack for short. Some people said he was mean as he could be; but I don't say that. He was fonder of scampering over the country than he was of helping his mother. Maybe he did n't know any better because he was n't taught any better. But one morning his mother was so

tired that she could n't get out of bed. She had
worn herself out with work. The next morning
she could n't get up, nor the next; and then the
neighbors, who had come in to see what the matter was, said that she would never get up any
more. So one day Johnny found everything very
still in the house, and the neighbors who were
there were kinder to him than they ever had been,
and then he knew that his mother would never
get tired any more.

"He felt so bad that he wandered off into the
woods, crying as he went. His eyes were so full
of tears that he could n't see where he was going,
and he did n't care. He went on and on, until,
finally, when he took heart to look around, he
found himself in a part of the country that was
new to him. This caused him to dry his eyes, for
he was perfectly sure that he had traveled neither
fast nor far enough to be beyond the limits of the
numberless journeys he had made in all directions
from his father's house; and yet, here he was,
suddenly and without knowing how he got there,
in a country that was altogether new to him.

"It was just like when you came down through
our spring gate," said Mr. Thimblefinger. "The

grass was different and the trees were different, and even the sand and the gravel were of a color that Johnny had never seen before. Suddenly, while he was wondering how he could have missed seeing all these strange things when he had journeyed this way before, a lady, richly dressed, came out of the woods and stood before him. She neither smiled nor looked severe, but pity seemed to shine in her face.

" 'What now?' she said, raising her hand to her head. 'You have come fast and come far. You are in trouble. Go back. When you want me, go to the Whispering Poplar that stands on the hill and call my name.'

" 'Who are you?' asked Johnny, forgetting to be polite, if he ever knew how.

" 'The Keeper of the Cows that roam in the night,' replied the lady. 'When you go to the Whispering Poplar that stands on the hill, whisper this : —

O Keeper of Cows that roam in the night,
Come over the hill and lend me your light.'

" Johnny would have thanked the woman, but in the twinkling of an eye she was gone without making a sound, and not a blade of grass shook to show that she had been there. Johnny turned in his tracks and started home the way he came. Before he had gone far he stopped to look back, but the strange country was nowhere to be seen — only the old familiar hills and trees that he had always known.

" When he got home there was a strange woman cooking and fixing his father's supper. The table was set, and everything was almost as neat and as tidy as it used to be when his mother was alive. Even his own little plate was in its place, and his mug, with the picture of a blue castle painted on it, was by the plate. But Johnny had no appetite. He went to the door and looked in, and then went to the stable. Once there, he suddenly remembered that he had forgotten to drive the cow in from the pasture. He went running to get her, but found her coming along of her own accord, something she was not in the habit of doing.

" Johnny wondered a little at this, but it soon passed out of his mind, and he got behind the cow and made her go faster. He drove the cow into the lot, and waited awhile for the woman to come and milk. But she delayed so long that he

A LADY, RICHLY DRESSED, CAME OUT OF THE WOODS

went to the house and found his father eating supper. Instead of going to the table, he went and sat by the fire.

"'Have something to eat?' said the woman.

"'I am not hungry,' he replied.

"'Have a glass of fresh milk, then?' she said.

"'Not to-night,' he answered. 'I have just driven the cow in from the pasture.'

"'I brought her from the pasture myself,' said the woman, 'milked her, and turned her out again.'

"Johnny said nothing to this, but he knew the cow had not been milked, and he wondered where the woman got the milk that his father was drinking. He thought it over, and forgot all about his grief. He noticed that as soon as his father drank the milk he began to smile at the woman. He smiled at the woman, but was cross to Johnny.

"After supper the woman went out, and after a while Johnny went out, too, leaving his father sitting by the fire smoking his pipe. Johnny went to the lot, thinking the woman had gone there. He wanted to see whether she would milk the cow. He crept along the side of the fence, and soon he was near enough to peep through a crack without being seen. He saw the woman rubbing the cow on the back while the calf was getting all the milk.

" ' You see how good I am to you, sister,' said she. 'Now I want you to be good to me. When that boy Jack goes after you to the pasture, I want you to lead him a chase. I saw him beating your calf to-day. But see how good I am to your calf, sister. I give it all the milk.'

"The cow shook her horn and switched her tail, and Johnny, sitting in the fence corner, wondered what it all meant.

" ' I see,' said the cow, after a while. ' You want to marry the boy's father, and the boy is in the way. But suppose they find you out. What then ? '

" ' Trust me for that, sister,' said the woman ; ' trust me for that.'

" Johnny waited to hear no more, but crept away and went to bed. He was dressed and out by sun-up next morning, but the woman was up before him, and had breakfast nearly ready. Johnny asked her if she had milked the cow, and she replied that she had milked and forgotten about it. Johnny saw the milk-pail setting on the shelf, and when he looked at it he knew the cow had not been milked, else the sides of the pail would have been spattered.

"But the cow had been turned out, and the calf was sleeping contentedly in the fence corner, instead of nibbling the grass. Johnny drank no milk at breakfast, but his father did, and smiled at the woman more than ever. During the day Johnny forgot all about the cow, but when night came he knew she must be brought up, so he went to the pasture after her. She was not to be found. He hunted over the hills and fields, and then, not finding her, began to cry.

"Suddenly the lady he had seen the day before stepped out of the wood and spoke to him. She held in her hand a tiny lantern.

"'Take this,' she said, holding out the lantern. 'You would n't call me, and so I came to you.'

"'I forgot,' whispered Johnny.

"'Don't forget any more,' said the lady. 'Take this lantern and run to the Whispering Poplar that stands on the hill. You 'll find your cow tied there. Drive her home, and don't spare her.'

"Johnny found the cow tied to the poplar sure enough, and he made her gallop home as fast as she could. He blew out his tiny lantern before he got in sight of the house, but it dropped from his hand and he could find it no more. He ceased to hunt for it after a while, and drove the cow to the lot, where the woman was waiting.

"'Go get your supper,' she said to Johnny.

"'Yes 'm,' replied Johnny, but he went off only to creep back to see what the woman would do.

"She abused the cow terribly. He could see that she was angry. 'You are a nice sister,' she exclaimed, 'to let that boy bring you home so early.'

"'Don't "sister" me,' moaned the cow. 'I'm nearly famished, and that boy has nearly run me off my legs. Somebody that I could n't see caught me and tied me to a tree this morning, and there I 've been all day. We 'd better go away from here. That boy will find you out yet.'

"Then Johnny crept away, ate his supper, and went to bed. He slept late the next morning, but when he awoke he found that his father, instead of being at work, as was his habit, was smoking his pipe and talking to the woman, and both were smiling at each other very sweetly. That afternoon, Johnny went to bring the cow home before sundown, but he could n't find her. He hunted and hunted for her until long after dark, and then he went to the Whispering Poplar that stands on the hill, and said : —

> " 'O Keeper of Cows that roam in the night,
> Come over the hills and lend me your light !'

" Instantly Johnny heard a cow lowing in the valley, and saw a light glimmering faintly in the distance. In a little while he heard a tremendous clatter of hoofs up the hill, and the rushing of some large animal through the bushes. It seemed to have one eye only and that eye shone as fiercely as a flame of fire as its head swayed from side to side. It came rushing to the poplar-tree where Johnny stood, and stopped there. Johnny peeped from behind the tree and saw that the frightful animal was nothing more than his cow, with a tiny lantern hanging on her horn. She stood there panting and trembling. Johnny waited to see if the Keeper of Cows that roam in the night would make her appearance, but he waited in vain.

Then he drove the cow home, turned her into the lot, and went in the house to get his supper. His father and the woman were sitting very close together.

"'Have you brought the cow?' the woman asked.

"'She's in the lot,' replied Johnny.

"'You are a smart boy,' said the woman.

"'Thanky, ma'am,' exclaimed Johnny.

"So it went on day after day. The woman would make the cow wander farther and farther away from home, and Johnny would go to the Whispering Poplar that stands on the hill and call for the beautiful lady, the Keeper of the Cows that roam in the night, and soon the cow would come running and lowing. Then Johnny would drive her home by the light of his little lantern. This happened so often that the neighbors, and indeed the people in all that country, when they saw a light bobbing around at night, would shake their heads and say, 'There goes Jack with his lantern,' and then after a while they called him 'Jack of the Lantern.'

"One day he heard two of the neighbors talking about him, saying it was a pity that so bright a boy should have such a stepmother as the woman his father was about to marry. Then Johnny (or Jack, as he was sometimes called) knew that his father was preparing to marry the woman who was keeping house for him, and it made the boy feel very wretched to think that this woman was to take the place of his mother.

" That very day he went to the Whispering Poplar that stands on the hill and called for the Keeper of the Cows that roam in the night. The lady made her appearance, and then Johnny told her his troubles. The lady smiled for the first time. Then she told Johnny that if he would follow her directions his troubles would disappear. She gave him a roll of blue ribbon, and told him what to say when he presented it to the woman just before the marriage took place. She told him also what to do with his little lantern. Johnny went home feeling very much better, and that night his father told him he was to have a new mother the next day. He said nothing in reply, but smiled as if the news pleased him.

" Johnny lay awake that night a long time, and once he thought the woman came and leaned over his bed as if to listen, but just then a cow not far away lowed once, twice, thrice.　Then the woman went away muttering something.

"The next day the invited guests began to assemble early, and after a while the preacher came. The women neighbors would have the bride to stand up in the middle of the floor to admire her just before the ceremony, and when she stood up Johnny began to march around her, waving his lantern and his blue ribbon and singing : —

> "' I have for the bride ten yards of blue ribbon —
>   Ten yards of blue ribbon, ten yards of blue ribbon —
> I have for the bride ten yards of blue ribbon,
>   So rich and so soft and so rare ;
> Five yards to pin on her snowy white bosom —
>   Her snowy white bosom, her snowy white bosom —
> Five yards to pin on her snowy white bosom,
>   And five to tie in her hair.
>
> "' I have a lantern to light her along with —
>   To light her along with, to light her along with —
> I have a lantern to light her along with,
>   When forth she fares in the night ;
> Out in the dark, the ribbon will rustle —
>   The ribbon will rustle, the ribbon will rustle —
> Out in the dark the ribbon will rustle,
>   And the lantern will lend her its light ! '

"Johnny threw the blue ribbon over the woman's shoulder and around her neck, and

waved his lantern, and instantly the woman disappeared, and in her place stood a cow. Before
the people could recover their surprise, the lady
that Johnny had seen aὶ the Whispering Poplar
came into the room and bowed to the company.

"'This is the most malicious cow in all my
herd,' said she, 'and this brave boy has caught
her. Here is a purse of gold for his reward. As
for you, sir,' turning to Johnny's father, 'you
may thank your son for saving you from this
witch.' Then she bowed again, and went away,
leading the cow, and neither of them was ever
seen in that country again.

"But to this day, when people see a light bobbing up and down in the fields at night, they say,
'Yonder's Jack of the Lantern!'"

X.

A LUCKY CONJURER.

"Now, I think that was a pretty good story," said Mr. Rabbit. "It had something about cows in it, and there was nothing about kings and princes. I would n't give *that*" — Mr. Rabbit blew a whiff of smoke from his mouth — "for all your princes and kings. Of course that 's on account of my ignorance. I don't know anything about them. I reckon they are just as good neighbors as anybody, when you come to know them right well."

Buster John laughed at this, but Sweetest Susan only smiled.

"Oh, I am not joking," remarked Mr. Rabbit solemnly. "There 's no reason why kings and queens and princes should n't be just as neighborly as other people. If a king and queen were keeping house anywhere near me, and were to send over after a mess of salad, or to borrow a cup of sugar or a spoonful of lard, I 'd be as ready to accommodate them as I would any other neighbors, and I reckon they 'd do the same by me."

" They 'd be mighty foolish if they did n't," said Mrs. Meadows.

" I hear tell dat folks hafter be monstus umble-come-tumble when dey go foolin' 'roun' whar dey er kingin' an' a queenin' at," remarked Drusilla. " Ef dey sont me fer ter borry any sugar er lard fum de house whar dey does de kingin' an' queenin', I boun' you I 'd stan' at the back gate an' holler 'fo' I went in dar whar dey wuz a-havin' der gwines on. Dey would n't git me in dar 'fo' I know'd how de lan' lay."

" I expect you are right, Tar Baby," replied Mr. Rabbit.

" Well, I 'm glad you did n't go to sleep over the story of the little boy and the lantern. But it did n't have any moral," said Mr. Thimble-finger.

" Why, I reckon that 's the reason I did n't do any nodding," explained Mr. Rabbit. " I knew there was something the matter."

There was a pause, during which Mr. Rabbit betrayed a tendency to fall to nodding again. Presently Mrs. Meadows remarked : —

"I mind me of a story that I heard once — I reckon the talk about kings and queens made me remember it. Anyway, it popped into my head all of a sudden, though I had n't thought about it in years."

"Fire away!" exclaimed Mr. Rabbit, opening his eyes and slowly closing them again.

"Once upon a time there lived in the land of Moraria a man who was very poor. He worked whenever and wherever he could find work, yet he had so many children that even if he had found work every day he could have made hardly enough for all to eat and wear. As it was, times were so hard and work was so scarce that he frequently had to go hungry and half clothed. His wife did the best she could, which was very little. She worked about the palace where the king had lived, but as she was only one among a hundred, she got small wages, and had few opportunities to carry any scraps of victuals to her children.

"Finally the man came to the conclusion that he must make a desperate effort to better his condition, so he said to his wife : —

"'What are my five senses for? I see other people living by their wits, and dressing fine and enjoying the best in the land. Why should n't I do the same? What is to prevent me but my stupidity?'

" 'Stupidity is a high fence to climb over,' replied the man's wife. 'But if you are willing to try how far your wits will carry you, you will have a good opportunity in a few days. The king's daughter, the Princess Myla, is to be married next week, and even now the guests are assembling at the palace — most of them belonging to the bridegroom's retinue.'

" The man leaned his head on his hand and thought a while, and then he rose and put on the best clothes he had, which were poor enough, and tied a rope girdle around his waist.

" 'I shall go to court as a pilgrim,' he said to his wife. 'When you see me, do you go around among the other servants and tell them that a great conjurer has arrived from the East. In this way it will come quickly to the King's ears. Nothing will come of that, but the next morning something valuable will be missing from the palace. When you hear of it, do you tell the rest that you know a man who can find whatever is missing.'

"'But how will you do this?' asked the woman.

"'Leave that to me,' he replied.

"The man carried out his plan, and his wife followed his directions. She pointed him out to her fellow-servants as a great conjurer from the East. Ragged as he was, the man stalked majestically about the palace-yard, and after a while sat on the ground with his face to the wall, and shook his head from side to side, and made many queer motions with his hands.

"Now, while the man sat there going through his queer motions, he heard voices on the other side of the wall. He judged that two men were resting in the shade on that side, and he knew by the way they talked that they had come with the young Prince who was to marry the Princess Myla.

"'You have left the blanket on the horse, I hope,' said one.

"'Yes, everything is attended to,' replied the other.

"'That is well,' remarked the first. 'The Prince, our master, desires the Princess Myla to be the first to look on this beautiful horse, which has just come out of Arabia. I will go myself to see that the animal is properly cared for.'

"Presently two strangers came through the gate, laughing and talking, and the man who was playing the conjurer knew they were the keepers of the horse. He rose when they went by, and watched them until he saw what part of the palace stables they entered. Then he slowly made his way out of the palace grounds.

"That night he went back and removed the horse, placing it where no one would be likely to find it. Then he told his wife what he had done.

"'There will be a great outcry,' said he, 'when the horse is missed. In the midst of it make your voice heard, and remind the young Prince's attendants that there is a famous conjurer within reach who can no doubt find the horse.'

"As the man said, so it turned out. There was a great noise made when it was found that the beautiful Arabian horse had been stolen. The young Prince was ready to tear his hair, so great was his disappointment. He offered a large sum of money to any one who would recover the horse. When the excitement was at its highest, the woman mentioned to some of the attendants that a famous conjurer had come to the palace. She then pointed her husband out to the men. At once the news was carried to the Prince, who was with the King.

" The King was not a believer in conjurers, and he quickly told the attendants to go send the vagabond about his business. But the young Prince was so keen to recover the beautiful horse which he had intended as a wedding gift for the Princess Myla that he insisted on consulting the conjurer. So the man was sent for. He came, followed by a number of people who were anxious to see what he would do. He had a very wise look as he bowed to the King and to the Prince.

" ' Who are you?' the King asked with a frown.

" ' A poor pilgrim,' your Majesty. ' Nothing more.'

" ' What is your business?'

" ' I am a student, your Majesty.'

" ' Where are your books?'

" ' In men's faces, your Majesty.'

" The man's replies were so apt that the King's ill-humor partly passed away.

"'A horse has been stolen from the royal stables,' said the King. 'I am told you are a conjurer. If you are, find the horse.'

"The man seated himself on the carpet, drew a crystal stone from his pocket, and asked the young Prince to warm it in the palm of his hand. Then the man took it and looked at it a few moments, rubbing his hand over it as if something blurred his sight. Then he said : —

"'The horse has on a blanket woven on a Russian loom. I see! A dapple-gray with milk-white mane and tail.'

"'That is the horse!' cried the Prince. 'Where is he?'

"'He is tied in a thicket a half league from here, near a road that leads to the river. He paws the ground and whinnies for his master. He is hungry.'

"At once messengers were sent and the horse found. The Prince was about to give the man a purse of gold, but the King stayed his hand, saying : —

"'I 'll test this fellow. I believe he is an imposter.'

"The man was very much frightened at this,

but there was no escape for him. The King went
to his private apartment, and shortly came back
with a covered basket in his hand.

"'There is a bird in this nest,' said the King.
'If you are a conjurer, tell me the name of
it.'

"'Alas, your Majesty,' cried the man, preparing to fall on his knees and beg for mercy, 'a
nest that would n't fit a sparrow might chance to
fit a crow.'

"'You certainly have gifts,' remarked the King
as he lifted the cover from the basket. As he
did so a crow hopped out and went stalking about
the room. The man was more astonished than
the King. In his fright he had hit on an old
saying that he had often heard, and it saved his
life.

"The Prince gave the man a purse of gold and
he was about to retire, when suddenly an attendant came running into the chamber crying that
some one had stolen the beautiful diamond ring
belonging to the Princess Myla.

"'Tell the Princess to trouble herself no further. We have here a man who will be able to
find it,' said the King.

AS HE DID SO, A CROW HOPPED OUT

"'Allow me a little time, your Majesty,' cried the man, who was now frightened nearly out of his wits. 'Let me go into a vacant room in a quiet part of the palace, where I may have an opportunity to look into this matter.'

"He was soon placed in a room near the servants' quarters, the attendants telling him that he would be summoned by the King in an hour. He went into the room, shut the door, and flung himself on the floor, bewailing his unhappy condition.

"Now the ring had been stolen by one of the women in attendance on the Princess. She was so pale and sad-looking that her companions had nicknamed her Misery, and sometimes the Princess herself, in a spirit of fun, called her by that name. She had heard how the conjurer had discovered the stolen horse, and she had seen him name the crow in the covered basket. Consequently she was very much frightened when she heard the King command him to find the stolen ring. She saw the conjurer go into the room, and after a while she crept to the door to listen, so great was her fear.

"The man in the room was not thinking of the

stolen ring at all.   He was merely bewailing his unhappy lot.

" 'Oh, misery, misery!' he cried; 'I have heard of you, but now I know you!'

" He had no sooner said this than there came a knock on the door and a voice said : —

" 'Don't talk so loud!   Open the door!'

" The man opened the door and saw a woman standing there trembling and weeping.

" 'Don't expose me,' she said, 'but spare my life.   I have the ring here.   I did wrong to steal it.'

" For a moment the man was so overcome with astonishment that he was unable to speak.   He took the ring in his hand and looked at it while the woman continued to plead with him.   He handed her the ring again.

" 'Take it,' he said, 'and place it beneath the corner of one of the rugs in the bedroom of the Princess.   Be quick about it, for I am going to the King.'

" The woman ran and did as she had been told, and then the man came from the room and sent an attendant to inform the King that the ring had been found.   The King sent for him.

" ' Where is the ring?'

" ' Under a corner of a rug in the bedroom of the Princess, your Majesty,' replied the man, bowing low and smiling.

"Search was at once made, and sure enough the beautiful ring was found under a corner of a rug in the Princess's bedroom. The Princess herself came to thank the conjurer, and if he had not been a very sensible man his head would have been turned by the attention he received. Even the King no longer doubted the conjurer's powers.

" ' There is something in this man,' said the King, and he straightway offered him a high position among his councilors.

" The man thanked the King most heartily, but declared that his business would not allow him to remain another day at court. So the King gave him a purse of gold, the young Prince gave him another, and the beautiful Princess Myla gave him a string of pearls of great value. Then he went home, bought him some land, built him a comfortable house, and went into business for himself.

" It sometimes happened that his wife complained because he did not accept the King's offer and remain at court, so that she might have flourished as a fine lady, but he always replied by saying that the man is a fool who will tempt Providence more than three times in a lifetime. Though he went into the palace poor and came out of it rich, he had escaped only by the skin of his teeth. He was always grateful for his good fortune, and by his example taught his children to lead virtuous lives and always to help the poor and needy."

XI.

THE KING OF THE CLINKERS.

CHICKAMY Crany Crow and Tickle-My-Toes had stopped frolicking, and were now listening to the stories. While Mrs. Meadows was telling about the lucky conjurer, Tickle-My-Toes became very uneasy. He moved about restlessly, pulled off his big straw hat, put it on again, and seemed to be waiting impatiently for the time to come when he might say something.

So, when Mrs. Meadows had finished, she looked at Tickle-My-Toes to see what he wanted. The rest did the same. But Tickle-My-Toes blushed very red, and looked at his feet.

"You acted as if you wanted to say something," said Mrs. Meadows, "and if you do, now's your chance. What's the matter? Have you run a splinter in your foot? You look as if you wanted to cry."

"I did want to say something," replied Tickle-My-Toes.

"What was it?" Mrs. Meadows inquired.

"Nothing much," answered Tickle-My-Toes, putting his finger in his mouth.

"I declare, I 'm ashamed of you," exclaimed Mrs. Meadows. "Here you are mighty near as old as I am, and yet trying to play boo-hoo baby."

"I don't think you ought to talk that way," said Tickle-My-Toes. "I thread your needles for you every day, and I do everything you ask me."

"I know what 's the matter with you," remarked Mrs. Meadows. "You want me to take you in my lap and rock you to sleep."

"Oh! I don't!" cried Tickle-My-Toes, blushing again. "I wanted to tell a story I heard, but I 'll go off somewhere and tell it to myself."

"There would n't be any fun in that," suggested Buster John.

"No," said Mrs. Meadows. "Tell the story right here, so we can enjoy it with you."

"You 'll laugh," protested Tickle-My-Toes.

"Not unless there 's something in the story to laugh at."

"This is no laughing story. It 's just as solemn as it can be," explained Tickle-My-Toes.

"Good!" exclaimed Mr. Rabbit. "If there 's anything I like, it is one of those solemn stories that make you feel like you want to go off behind the house and shake hands with yourself, and cry boo-hoo to the ell-and-yard and seven stars."

Mr. Rabbit's enthusiastic remark was very encouraging to Tickle-My-Toes, who, after scratching his head a little, and looking around to see if he could find a place to hide when the time came, began his story in this wise: —

"Once upon a time, and in a big town away off yonder somewhere, there lived a little boy who had no father nor mother. He was so small that nobody seemed to care anything about him. But one day a woman, the wife of a baker, heard him crying in the streets, and carried him into the house, and gave him something to eat, and warmed him by the fire, and after that he felt better.

"The baker himself grumbled a great deal when he came home and found what his wife had done. He said he would n't be surprised to come home some day and find his house full of other people's children. But his wife replied that it would be well enough to complain when he found the house full. As for this little brat, she said, he would n't fill a milk jar if he was put in it, much less a great big house.

"The baker growled and grumbled, but his wife paid no attention to him. She sat in her chair and rocked and sang, and was just as good-natured as she could be. After a while the baker himself got over his grumbling, and began to laugh. He told his wife that he had sold all his bread that day, and had orders for as much the next day.

"'Of course,' said she; 'but if I had left that child crying in the streets your business would have been ruined before the year is out.'

"'Maybe so,' replied the baker.

"Well, the little boy grew very fast, and was as lively as a cricket. The baker's wife thought as much of him as if he had been her own son, and the baker himself soon came to be very fond of him. He was very smart, too. He learned to watch the fire under the big oven, and to make himself useful in many ways. He played about the oven so much, and was so fond of watching the bread bake and the fire burn, that the baker's wife called him Sparkle Spry.

"For many years the country where the baker

and his wife and Sparkle Spry lived had been at peace with all the other countries. But one day a man from a neighboring country had his nose pulled by somebody in the baker's country, and then war was declared by the kings and queens, and the people fell to fighting.

"Now, when people fight they must be fed, and the cheapest thing to feed them on is bread. A part of the army camped near the town where the baker lived, and there was a great demand for bread. The baker's oven was not a large one, and by running it day and night he could only bake three hundred loaves.

"He and his wife baked until they were tired out. They told Sparkle Spry to watch the oven so that the bread would n't burn, and to wake them when it was brown. They were so tired that Sparkle Spry was sorry for them, and he wondered why he was n't big enough to take their places, if only for one day and night. While he was thinking and wishing, he saw something moving. He rubbed his eyes and looked again, and then he saw an old man, no bigger than a broomstick, and no taller than a teacup, peeping from behind the oven.

"'Are they all gone?' he whispered, coming forward a little way.

"'All who?' asked Sparkle Spry.

"'The old ones — the big man and the fat woman.'

"'They have gone to bed,' said Sparkle Spry. 'I can call them!'

"'No, no,' cried the old man. 'They are such fools! They don't know what is good for them. I have been waiting for years to get a chance to show them how to bake bread. Once I showed myself to the man, and he thought I was a snake; once to the woman, and she thought I was a rat. What fools they are!'

"'Who are you?' inquired Sparkle Spry. He did n't like to hear his friends abused.

"'Who — me? I'm the King of the Clinkers — twice plunged in the water and twice burned in the fire.'

"'Well, to-night you can bake all the bread you want to,' said Sparkle Spry. 'The baker and his wife have been trying to supply the army that is camped here, but their oven is too small. They have worked until they can work no longer, and now they have gone to bed to rest.'

HE SAW AN OLD MAN, NO BIGGER THAN A BROOMSTICK

"'Good!' cried the King of the Clinkers. 'Shut the door, so they can't hear us! I'll show them a thing or two about baking bread.'

"Then he walked close to the hot oven, tapped on it with a little poker that he carried in his belt, and called out: 'Wake up! Get out! Come on! Hurry up! We've no time to lose! Show yourselves! Stir about! Be lively!'

"With that, hundreds of little men swarmed out of the ash heap behind the oven, some of them sneezing and some rubbing their eyes, but all jumping about with motions as quick as those of a flea when he jumps.

"Oh, please don't talk about fleas," pleaded Mr. Rabbit, shuddering and scratching himself behind the ear. "It makes the cold chills run up my back. I never hear 'em named but I think I can feel 'em crawling on me."

"Anyhow, that's the way the little men jumped about," said Tickle-My-Toes, resuming his story. "They swarmed in and out of the oven, hot as it was; they swarmed in and out of the flour barrels; they swarmed in and out of the trough where the dough was kneaded; and they swarmed in and out of the woodshed.

" The King of the Clinkers stood sometimes on the edge of the oven, sometimes on the edge of the flour barrels, sometimes on the edge of the trough, sometimes on the woodpile, and sometimes at the door of the furnace. And wherever he stood he waved his tiny poker and told the others what to do.

"Some of the little men carried wood to the furnace, some carried flour and water to the trough, some carried dough to the oven, and some brought out the hot and smoking bread. Sparkle Spry watched all this with so much surprise that he did n't know what to say or do. He saw the loaves of bread rise up in rows as high as the ceiling, and he sat and watched it as dumb as an oyster. He had seen bread baked, but he had never seen such baking as this.

" Finally the eye of the King of the Clinkers fell on Sparkle Spry. ' Don't sit there doing nothing,' he cried. ' Go fetch wood and pile it here by the furnace door. You can do that ! '

"Sparkle Spry did as he was bid, but though he brought the wood as fast as he could, he found that he could n't bring it fast enough. Pretty soon the King of the Clinkers called out to him :

" 'You can rest now. The flour is all gone, and we have hardly begun.'

" 'There 's plenty in the storehouse,' said Sparkle Spry.

" 'How many barrels?' asked the King of the Clinkers.

" 'Two hundred,' Sparkle Spry answered.

" The King of the Clinkers wrung his hands in despair. 'Hardly a mouthful — hardly a mouthful! It will all be gone before the chickens crow for day. But run fetch the key. Two hundred barrels will keep us busy while they last.'

" Sparkle Spry brought the key of the storehouse door, and the little men swarmed in and rolled the barrels out in a jiffy. Only one accident happened. In taking the flour out of one of the barrels, after they had rolled it near the dough trough, one of the little men fell in and would have been drowned but for Sparkle Spry, who felt around in the loose flour and lifted him out."

" Drowned!" cried Sweetest Susan.

" Of course," answered Tickle-My-Toes. "Why not? I ought to have said 'smothered,' but now that I 've said 'drowned' I 'll stick to it."

"Better stick to the story," remarked Mr. Rabbit solemnly, — "better stick to the story."

"Now, I think he 's doing very well," said Mrs. Meadows in an encouraging tone.

"Well," said Tickle-My-Toes, "the little men worked away until they had baked the two hundred barrels of flour into nice brown loaves of bread. This made five hundred barrels they had used, and that was all the baker had on hand. The fifteen hundred pounds of flour made twenty hundred and odd fat loaves, and these the King of the Clinkers had carried into the storehouse.

"When all this was done, and nicely done, the King of the Clinkers went to the door of the room where the baker and his wife were sleeping. They were snoring as peacefully as two good people ever did. Then he went to the street door and listened.

"'Get home — get home!' he cried to the little men. 'I hear wagons rumbling on the pavement; they will be here presently for bread.'

"The little men scampered this way and that, behind the oven and into the ash heap, and, in a few seconds, all had disappeared.

"'Now,' said the King of the Clinkers, 'I want

to tell you that I 've had a splendid time, and I 'm very much obliged to you for it. I have enjoyed myself, and I want to make some returns for it. Pretty soon the bread wagons will be at the door clamoring for bread. You will wake the baker and his wife. When they find all their flour made into nice bread they will be very much surprised. They will ask you who did it. You must tell them the truth. They will not believe it, but they 'll be very proud of you. They will be willing to give you anything you want. Tell them you want a wooden horse. They will have it built for you. It must have a window on each side and good strong hinges in the legs. Good-by! I hear the wagons at the door.'

"The King of the Clinkers waved his hand and disappeared behind the oven. The wagons rattled near the door, the teamsters cracking their whips and calling for bread for the hungry army. Sparkle Spry ran to the baker and shook him, and ran to the baker's wife and shook her. They were soon awake, but when the baker learned that the wagons had come for bread, he threw up both hands in despair.

"'I 'm ruined!' he cried. 'I ought to have

been baking and here I 've been sleeping! And
the army marches away to-day, leaving me with
all my stock of flour on hand. Oh, why did n't
the boy wake me?'

" 'Come,' said his wife; ' we 'll sell what we 've
got, and not cry over the rest.'

" They went into the storehouse, and there they
saw a sight such as they had never seen before.
The room was so full of steaming bread that they
could hardly squeeze in at the door. From floor
to ceiling it was stacked and packed. They sold
and sold until every loaf was gone, and then, instead of the bread, the baker and his wife had a
sack full of silver money.

" The baker went in to count it, but his wife
took it away from him. ' Not now,' she said;
' not until we have thanked this boy.'

" 'You are right!' cried the baker. ' It 's the
most wonderful thing I ever heard of. How did
you manage it?'

" 'Some little men helped me,' answered Sparkle Spry.

" The woman seized his hands and kissed his
fingers. ' These are the little men,' she exclaimed.

"'There 's one thing I 'm sorry for,' said Sparkle Spry.

"'What is that?' asked the baker.

"'Why, we had to burn so much wood.'

"'Don't mention it — don't mention it,' protested the baker.

"'Now,' said the baker's wife, embracing Sparkle Spry again, 'you deserve something for making us rich. What shall it be?'

"The baker frowned a little at this, but his brow cleared when Sparkle Spry replied that he wanted a wooden horse built.

"'You shall have it,' said the baker's wife.

"'Yes, indeed,' assented the baker. 'As fine a one as you want.'"

XII.

W HEN Tickle-My-Toes had told about how
pleased the baker and his wife were with Sparkle
Spry, he paused and looked at Chickamy Crany
Crow, as if he expected that she would beckon
him away.   But, instead of that, she said: —

"Why, that is n't all."

"Well, it 's enough, I hope," replied Tickle-
My-Toes.

"No," said Mrs. Meadows, "it 's not enough,
if there 's any more.   Why, so far it 's the best
of all the stories.   It 's new to me.   I had an idea
that I had heard all the stories, but this one is a
pole over my persimmon, as we used to say in the
country next door."

"I don't like to tell stories," protested Tickle-
My-Toes, puckering his face in a comical way.
"It 's too confining."

"Nonsense!" exclaimed Mr. Rabbit.   "It 's
time you were settling down.   What will you look

like a year or two from now, if you keep on cutting up your capers?"

Tickle-My-Toes caught hold of the corner of Chickamy Crany Crow's apron, and, thus fortified, resumed his story:—

"Well, the baker and his wife promised Sparkle Spry they would have him a big wooden horse made, and they were as good as their word. They sent right off that very day for a carpenter and joiner, and when he came, Sparkle Spry showed the man what he wanted. He said the horse must be as much like a real horse as could be made out of wood, and three times as big.

"The man asked the baker's wife what the brat wanted with such a machine as that, and this made the good woman mad.

"'He's no brat, I can tell you that!' she exclaimed, 'and if he wants a play horse as big as a whale and the same shape, he shall have it. Now if you want to make his play horse, get to work and make it. If not, I'll get somebody else to make it.'

"But the man declared he meant no harm, and said he was glad to get the work. So he got the lumber, and in a few days, being a very clever workman, he had finished the wooden horse. He made it just as Sparkle Spry wanted him to. He put big hinges at the joints of the legs, cut a window in each side of the body, made the ears and the nostrils hollow, and fixed pieces of glass for the eyes.

"The carpenter seemed to enjoy his work, too, for every time he went off a little distance to see how his work looked, he laughed as hard as he could. When he was nearly done he asked Sparkle Spry if he wanted the roof shingled.

"'Why, no,' replied the boy. 'There's no roof there. Besides, horses don't have shingles on them.'

"He'll look pretty rough," remarked the man.

"'Yes,' said Sparkle Spry, 'but after you get through with him he is to be polished off.'

"'That's so,' the carpenter assented, 'but this horse has a good many things about him that other horses have n't got.'

"So, when the carpenter was through with the horse, a leather finisher was sent for, and he covered the horse with hides of cows tanned with the hair on, and fixed a cow's tail where the horse's tail should have been.

"The baker grumbled a little at this extra expense, and said he was afraid Sparkle Spry had strained his head the night he baked so much bread. But the baker's wife said she would like to have a whole house full of crazy children, if Sparkle Spry was crazy.

"When the wooden horse was finished, Sparkle Spry waited until the baker and his wife had gone to bed, and then he tapped on the oven and whistled. Presently the King of the Clinkers peeped out to see what the matter was. He came from behind the oven cautiously, until he found that Sparkle Spry was alone, and then he came forth boldly.

"'The horse is ready,' said Sparkle Spry.

"'Ready!' exclaimed the King of the Clinkers. 'Well, I think it is high time. My workmen could have built it in a night; and here I have been waiting and waiting for I don't know how long.'

"'I hope you 'll like it,' Sparkle Spry suggested.

"'Like it!' cried the King of the Clinkers. 'Why, of course I 'll like it. I have n't enjoyed a ride in so long that I 'm not likely to quarrel with the horse that carries me.'

" 'But this is a wooden horse,' remarked Sparkle Spry.

" 'I should hope so; yes, indeed!' grunted the King of the Clinkers. 'I have been riding wooden horses as long as I can remember. They may be a little clumsy, but they suit me.'

" 'But this horse has no rockers,' persisted Sparkle Spry. 'It is as solid as a house.'

" 'Much you know about wooden horses,' said the King of the Clinkers. 'Wait; I 'll call my torchbearers.'

" He tapped on the oven with his tiny poker, and immediately a company of little men filed out from behind it. As they passed the furnace door they lit their torches at a live coal, and marched out to the wooden horse, followed by the King of the Clinkers and Sparkle Spry.

" The latter had reason to be very much astonished at what he saw then and afterwards. The torchbearers led the way to the left foreleg of the wooden horse, opened a door, and filed up a spiral stairway, the King of the Clinkers following after. Sparkle Spry climbed up by means of a stepladder that the carpenter had used. When he crawled through the window in the side of the wooden horse, he saw that a great transformation had taken place, and the sight of it almost took his breath away.

" A furnace with a small bake oven had been fitted up, and there was also a supply of flour, coal, and wood. The flue from the furnace ran in the inside of the horse's neck, finding a vent for the smoke at the ears. On all sides were to be seen the tools and furniture of a bakery, and there were places where the little men might stow themselves away when they were not on duty, and there was a special apartment for the King of the Clinkers.

" In a little while the whole interior of the horse swarmed with the followers of the King of the Clinkers, who stood counting them as they came in.

" ' All here,' he said, waving his little poker. ' Now get to bed and rest yourselves.'

" They complied so promptly that they seemed to disappear as if by magic. The torchbearers had thrown their torches in the furnace, and as wood had already been placed there, a fire was soon kindled.

" ' Now,' said the King of the Clinkers, closing

the draught, ' we 'll let it warm up a little and see if the carpenter has done his work well.'

" Thereupon he pulled a cord that seemed to be tied to a bell, and, in a little while, Sparkle Spry felt that the horse was in motion. He hardly knew what to make of it. He went to the window and peeped out, and the lights in the houses seemed to be all going to the rear. Occasionally a creaking sound was heard, and sometimes he could feel a jar or jolt in the horse's frame.

" ' Are we flying?' he asked, turning to the King of the Clinkers.

" ' Flying! Nothing of the sort. Don't you feel a jolt when the horse lifts up a foot and puts it down again? I 'm mighty glad it is a pacing horse. If it was a trotting horse it would shake us all to pieces.'

" ' Where are we going?' inquired Sparkle Spry.

" ' Following the army — following the army,' replied the King of the Clinkers. ' There 's going to be a big battle not far from here, and we may take a hand in it. The king of the country is a fat old rascal, and is n't very well thought of by the rest of the kings, who are his cousins; but I live here, and he has never bothered me. Consequently, I don't mind helping him out in a pinch.'

"'How far do you have to go?' asked Sparkle Spry, who had no great relish for war if it was as hard as he had heard it was.

"'Oh, a good many miles,' replied the King of the Clinkers, 'and we are not getting on at all. There's not enough mutton suet on the knee hinges to suit me.'

"So saying, he struck the bell twice, and instantly Sparkle Spry could feel that the wooden horse was going faster.

"'Does the horse go by the road or through the fields?' asked Sparkle Spry.

"'Oh, we take short cuts when necessary,' answered the King of the Clinkers. 'We have no time to go round by the road. I hope you are not scared.'

"'No, not scared,' replied Sparkle Spry somewhat doubtfully; 'but it makes me feel queer to be traveling through the country in a wooden horse.'

"Nothing more was said for some time, and

Sparkle Spry must have dropped off to sleep, for suddenly he was aroused by the voice of the King of the Clinkers, who called out: —

" 'Here we are! Get up! Stir about!'

"Sparkle Spry jumped to his feet and looked from the window. Day was just dawning, and on the plain before him he saw hundreds of twinkling lights, as if a shower of small stars had fallen to the ground during the night. Being somewhat dazed by his experiences, he asked what they were.

" 'Camp-fires,' replied the King of the Clinkers. 'The army that we are going to attack is camped further away, but if you will lift your eyes a little, you will see their camp-fires.'

" 'Do we attack them by ourselves?' Sparkle Spry asked.

" 'Of course!' the King of the Clinkers answered. 'I never did like too much company; besides, I want you to get the credit of it.'

" 'Now, I 'd rather be certain of a whole skin than to have any credit,' protested Sparkle Spry.

"But the King of the Clinkers paid no attention to his protests. He gave his orders to his little men, and strutted about with an air of importance that Sparkle Spry would have thought comical if he had not been thinking of the battle.

"Daylight came on and drowned out the camp-fires, leaving only thin columns of blue smoke to mark them. The wooden horse moved nearer and nearer to the army directly in front of them, and finally came close to the headquarters of the commanding general, who sent out a soldier to inquire the meaning of the apparition. Finally the general came himself, accompanied by his staff, and to him Sparkle Spry repeated what the King of the Clinkers had told him to say. The general pulled his mustache and knitted his brows mightily, and finally he said : —

"'I'm obliged to you for coming. You'll have to do the best you can. I never have commanded a wooden horse, and if I were to tell you what to do, I might get you into trouble. I'll just send word along the line that the wooden horse is on our side, and you'll have to do the best you can.'

"As he said, so he did. The army soon knew that a big wooden horse had come to help it, and when the queer looking machine moved to the front, the soldiers got out of the way as fast as they could, and some of them forgot to carry their arms with them. But order was soon restored, and presently it was seen that the opposing army was marching forward to begin the battle.

"The King of the Clinkers waited until the line was formed, and then he sounded the little bell. The horse started off. The bell rang twice, and the horse went faster. Sparkle Spry, looking from the window, could see that he was going at a tremendous rate. The horse went close to the opposing army, and then turned and went down the line to the left. Turning, it came up the line, this time very close. Turning again, it came back, and the soldiers in the front line were compelled to scamper out of the way. While this was going on, the other army came up, but by the time it arrived on the battle-ground there was nothing to fight.

"The wooden horse had stampeded the enemy's army, and the soldiers had all run away, leaving their arms, their tents, and their bread wagons to be captured.

"The commanding general of the victorious army thanked Sparkle Spry very heartily. 'I 'll mention your name in my report to the king,' he

THE WOODEN HORSE HAD STAMPEDED THE ENEMY'S ARMY

said. 'But I hardly know what to say about the affair. You would n't call this a battle, would you?'

" 'No,' replied Sparkle Spry, 'I saw no signs of a battle where I went along.'

" 'It is very curious,' said the general. 'I don't know what we are coming to. A great victory, but nobody killed and no prisoners taken.'

" Then he went off to write his report, and some time afterward the king sent for Sparkle Spry, and gave him lands and houses and money, and made him change his every-day name for a high-sounding one. And the baker and his wife came to live near him, and the King of the Clink-ers used to come at night with all his little men, and they had a very good time after all, in spite of the high-sounding name."

With this, Tickle-My-Toes turned and ran away as hard as he could, whereupon Mr. Rabbit opened his eyes and asked in the most solemn way : —

"Is there a wooden horse after him? I wish you 'd look."

XIII.

HOW BROTHER LION LOST HIS WOOL.

Mr. Rabbit shaded his eyes with his hand, and
pretended to believe that there might be a wooden
horse trying to catch Tickle-My-Toes after all.
But Mrs. Meadows said that there was no danger
of anything like that. She explained that Tickle-
My-Toes was running away because he did n't
want to hear what was said about his story.

"I think he 's right," remarked Mr. Rabbit.
"It was the queerest tale I ever heard in all my
life. You might sit and listen to tales from now
until — well — until the first Tuesday before the
last Saturday in the year seven hundred thousand,
seven hundred and seventy-seven, and you 'd
never hear another tale like it."

"I don't see why," suggested Mrs. Meadows.

"Well," replied Mr. Rabbit, chewing his to-
bacco very slowly, "there are more reasons than
I have hairs in my head, but I 'll only give you
three. In the first place, this Sparkle Spry does n't

marry the king's daughter. In the second place, he does n't live happily forever after; and in the third place " — Mr. Rabbit paused and scratched his head — " I declare, I 've forgotten the third reason."

" If it 's no better than the other two, it does n't amount to much," said Mrs. Meadows. " There 's no reason why he should n't have married the king's daughter, if the king had a daughter, and if he did n't live happily it was his own fault. Stories are not expected to tell everything."

" Now, I 'm glad of that," exclaimed Mr. Rabbit, " truly glad. I 've had a story on my mind for many years, and I 've kept it to myself because I had an idea that in telling a story you had to tell everything."

" Well, you were very much mistaken," said Mrs. Meadows with emphasis.

" So it seems — so it seems," remarked Mr. Rabbit.

" What was the story? " asked Buster John.

" I called it a story," replied Mr. Rabbit, " but that is too big a name for it. I reckon you have heard of the time when Brother Lion had hair all over him as long and as thick as the mane he now has? "

But the children shook their heads. They had never heard of that, and even Mrs. Meadows said it was news to her.

"Now, that is very queer," remarked Mr. Rabbit, filling his pipe slowly and deliberately. "Very queer, indeed. Time and again I 've had it on the tip of my tongue to mention this matter, but I always came to the conclusion that everybody knew all about it. Of course it does n't seem reasonable that Brother Lion went about covered from head to foot, and to the tip of his tail, with long, woolly hair; but, on the other hand, when he was first seen without his long, woolly hair, he was the laughing-stock of the whole district. I know mighty well he was the most miserable looking creature I ever saw.

"It was curious, too, how it happened," Mr. Rabbit continued. "We were all living in a much colder climate than that in the country next door. Six months in the year there was ice in the river and snow on the ground, and them that did n't lay up something to eat when the weather was open had a pretty tough time of it the rest of the year. Brother Lion's long woolly hair belonged to the climate. But for that, he would have frozen to death, for he was a great hunter, and he had to be out in all sorts of weather.

" One season we had a tremendous spell of cold weather, the coldest I had ever felt. I happened to be out one day, browsing around, when I saw blue smoke rising a little distance off, so I says to myself, says I, I 'll go within smelling distance of the fire and thaw myself out. I went towards the smoke, and I soon saw that Mr. Man, who lived not far off, had been killing hogs.

" Now, the funny thing about that hog-killing business," continued Mr. Rabbit, leaning back in his chair and smacking his lips together, as old people will do sometimes, "was that, after the hogs were killed, Mr. Man had to get their hair off. I don't know how people do now, but that was what Mr. Man did then. He had to get the hair off — but how? Well, he piled up wood, and in between the logs he placed rocks and stones. Then he dug a hole in the ground and half buried a hogshead, the open end tilted up a little higher than the other end. This hogshead he filled with as much water as it would hold in that position. Then he set fire to the pile of wood. As it burned, of course the rocks would become heated. These Mr. Man would take in a shovel and throw in the hogshead of water. The hot rocks would heat the water, and in this way the hogs were scalded so the hair on their hides could be scraped off.

"Well, the day I 'm telling you about, Mr. Man had been killing hogs and scalding the hair off. When I got there the pile of wood had burned away, and Mr. Man had just taken his hogs home in his wagon. The weather was very cold, and as I stood there warming myself I heard Brother Lion roaring a little way off. He had scented the fresh meat, and I knew he would head right for the place where the hogs had been killed.

"Now, Brother Lion had been worrying me a good deal. He had hired Brother Wolf to capture me, and Brother Wolf had failed. Then he hired Brother Bear, and Brother Bear got into deep trouble. Finally he hired Brother Fox, and I knew the day was n't far off when Mrs. Fox would have to hang crape on her door and go in mourning. All this had happened some time before, and I bore Brother Lion no good will.

" So, when I heard him in the woods singing out that he smelled fresh blood, I grabbed the shovel the man had left, and threw a dozen or so hot rocks in the hogshead, and then threw some fresh dirt on the fire. Presently Brother Lion came trotting up, sniffing the air, purring like a spinning wheel a-running, and dribbling at the mouth.

" I passed the time of day with him as he came up, but kept further away from him than he could jump. He seemed very much surprised to see me, and said it was pretty bad weather for such little chaps to be out; but I told him I had on pretty thick underwear, and besides that I had just taken a hot bath in the hogshead.

" 'I 'm both cold and dirty,' says he, smelling around the hogshead, 'and I need a bath. I 've been asleep in the woods yonder, and I 'm right stiff with cold. But that water is bubbling around in there mightily.'

" 'I 've just flung some rocks in,' says I.

" 'How do you get in ?' says he.

" 'Back in,' says I.

" Brother Lion walked around the hogshead once or twice, as if to satisfy himself that there was no trap, and then he squatted and began to crawl into the hogshead backwards. By the time his hind leg touched the water, he pulled it out with a howl, and tried to jump away, but, somehow, his foot slipped off the rim of the hogshead, and he soused into the water — kerchug! — up to his shoulders."

Mr. Rabbit paused, shut his eyes, and chuckled to himself.

" Well, you never heard such howling since you were born. Brother Lion scrambled out quicker than a cat can wink her left eye, and rolled on the ground, and scratched around, and tore up the earth considerably. I thought at first he was putting on and pretending; but the water must have been mighty hot, for while Brother Lion was scuffling around, all the wool on his body came off up to his shoulders, and if you were to see him to-day you 'd find him just that way.

" And more than that — before he soused himself in that hogshead of hot water, Brother Lion used to strut around considerably. Being the king of all the animals, he felt very proud, and he used to go with his tail curled over his back.

YOU NEVER HEARD SUCH HOWLING SINCE YOU WERE BORN

But since that time, he sneaks around as if he was afraid somebody would see him.

"There 's another thing. His hide hurt him so bad for a week that every time a fly lit on him he 'd wiggle his tail. Some of the other animals, seeing him do this, thought it was a new fashion, and so they began to wiggle their tails. Watch your old house cat when you go home, and you will see her wiggle her tail forty times a day without any reason or provocation. Why? Simply because the other animals, when they saw Brother Lion wiggling his tail, thought it was the fashion; and so they all began it, and now it has become a habit with the most of them. It is curious how such things go.

"But the queerest thing of all," continued Mr. Rabbit, leaning back in his chair, and looking at Mrs. Meadows and the children through half-closed eyes, "was this — that the only wool left on Brother Lion's body, with the exception of his mane, was a little tuft right on the end of his tail."

"How was that?" inquired Mrs. Meadows.

Mr. Rabbit laughed heartily, but made **no** reply.

" I don't see anything to laugh at," said Mrs. Meadows with some emphasis. " A civil question deserves a civil answer, I 've always heard."

" Well, you know what you said a while ago," remarked Mr. Rabbit.

" I don't know as I remember," replied Mrs. Meadows.

" Why, you said pointedly that it was not necessary to tell everything in a story." Mr. Rabbit made this remark with great dignity. "And I judged by the way you said it that it was bad taste to tell everything."

" Oh, I remember now," said Mrs. Meadows, laughing. " It was only one of my jokes."

" But this is no joke," protested Mr. Rabbit, winking at the children, but keeping the serious side of his face toward Mrs. Meadows. " I took you at your solemn word. Now there is a tuft of wool on Brother Lion's tail, and you ask me how it happened to be there. I answer you as you answered me — 'You don't have to tell everything in a story.' Am I right, or am I wrong ?"

" I 'll not dispute with you," remarked Mrs. Meadows, taking up her knitting.

" I don't mind telling you," remarked Mr. Rabbit, turning to the children with a confidential air. " It was as simple as falling off a log. When Brother Lion fell into the hogshead of hot water, the end of his tail slipped through the bung-hole."

This explanation was such an unexpected one that the children laughed, and so did Mrs. Meadows. But Mr. Thimblefinger, who had put in an appearance, shook his head and remarked that he was afraid that Mr. Rabbit got worse as he grew older, instead of better.

XIV.

"The fact is," remarked Mr. Rabbit, "I was just telling the story — if you can call it a story — to please company. If you think the end of Brother Lion's tale is the end of the story, well and good; but it did n't stop there when I told it in my young days. And it did n't stop there when it happened. But maybe I 've talked too long and said too much. You know how we gabble when we get old."

"I like to hear you talk," said Sweetest Susan, edging a little closer to Mr. Rabbit and smiling cutely.

Mr. Rabbit took off his glasses and wiped them on his big red handkerchief.

"There 's some comfort in that," he declared. "If you really like to hear me talk, I'll go right ahead and tell the rest of the story. It 's a little rough in spots, but you 'll know how to make allowances for that. The creatures had claws and tushes, and where these grow thick and long, there's bound to be more or less scratching and biting.

"Of course, when Brother Lion had the wool scalded off his hide, he was in a pretty bad condition. He managed to get home, but it was a long time before he could come out and go roaming around the country. As he was the king of the animals, of course all the rest of the creatures called on him to see how he was getting on. I did n't go myself, because I did n't know how he felt towards me. I was afraid he had heard me laugh when he backed into the hogshead of hot water, though I made believe I was sneezing. Consequently, I did n't go and ask him how he was getting on.

"But I went close enough to know that Brother Fox had told Brother Lion a great rigamarole about me. That was Brother Fox's way. In front of your face, he was sweeter than sauce and softer than pudding, but behind your back — well, he did n't have any claws, but what tushes he had he showed them.

"I never did hear what Brother Fox said about me in any one place and at any one time, but I heard a little here and a little there, and when **it** was all patched up and put together it made a great mess. I had done this, and I had done that; I had laughed at Brother Lion behind his back, and I had snickered at him before his face; I had talked about him and made fun of him; and, besides all that, I had never had the politeness to call on him.

"All the other animals found Brother Lion so willing to listen that they learned Brother Fox's lies by heart, and went and recited them here and there about the country; and in that way I got hold of the worst of them. The trouble with Brother Fox was that he had an old grudge against me. He had been trying to outdo me for many a long year, but somehow or other he always got caught in his own trap. He had a willing mind and a thick head, and when these get together there's always trouble. The willing mind pushes and the thick head goes with its eyes shut.

"In old times, people used to say that Brother Fox was cunning, but I believe they've quit that since the facts have come to light. My experience with him is that he is blessed with about as much sense as a half-grown guinea pig. He's a pretty swift runner, but he does n't even know when the time comes to run.

"Of course, when Brother Fox found out that for some reason or other I was n't visiting Brother Lion, he seized the chance to talk about me, and it was n't such a great while before he managed to make Brother Lion believe that I was the worst enemy he had and the cause of all his trouble.

" I knew pretty well that something of the sort was going on, for every time I 'd meet any of the other animals, they 'd ask me why I did n't call and see Brother Lion. Brother Fox, especially, was anxious to know why I had n't gone to ask after Brother Lion's health.

"I put them all off for some time, until finally one day I heard that Brother Lion had given Brother Fox orders to catch me and bring me before him. This did n't worry me at all, because I knew that Brother Fox was just as able to catch me as I was to catch a wild duck in the middle of a mill-pond. But I concluded I 'd go and see Brother Lion and find out all about his health.

"So I went, taking good care to go galloping by Brother Fox's house. He was sitting on his front porch, and I could see he was astonished, but I neither said howdy nor turned my head. I knew he would follow along after.

"When I got to Brother Lion's house every-thing was very quiet, but I knew Brother Lion was awake, for I heard him groan every time he tried to turn over. So I rapped at the door and then walked in. Brother Lion watched me from under his touseled mane for some time before he said anything. Then he says, says he:—

"'What's this I hear?'

"Says I, 'Not having your ears, I can't say.'

"'My ears are as good as anybody's ears,' says he.

"'But I can't hear through them,' says I.

"He grunted and grumbled a little over this, because he did n't know what reply to make.

"'You have n't been to see me until now,' says he.

"'No,' says I; 'I knew you were pretty bad off, and so I had no need to come and ask you how you were. I knew I was partly to blame in the matter, and so I went off to see if I could n't find a cure for you.'

"Says he, 'Don't talk about cures. Every-body that has come to see me has a cure. I 've tried 'em all, and now I 'm worse off than I was at first.'

"Says I, 'I could have come as often as Brother Fox did, and my coming would have done you just as much good.'

"'I don't know about that,' says he. 'Brother Fox has been mighty neighborly. He has lost sleep on my account, and he has told me a great many things that I did n't know before.'

"'Likely enough,' says I. 'I 've known him to tell people a great many things that he did n't know himself. But Brother Fox,' says I, 'was the least of all things in my mind when I found out that you had been scalded by water that was not more than milk-warm. I did n't need to be told that when milk-warm water scalds the hair off of anybody, something else is the matter beside the scalding.'

"At this Brother Lion seemed to quiet down a little. He did n't talk so loud, and he began to show the whites of his eyes.

"'Yes,' says I, 'Brother Fox is famous for talking behind the door, but I 've noticed that he never says anything nice about anybody. You know what he 's said about me, but do you know what he's said about you?   Of course you don't, and I'm not going to tell you, because I don't want you to be worried.'

"'But I'd like to know,' says Brother Lion, says he.

"'It wouldn't do you any good,' says I. 'I could have come here and jowered and made a good deal of trouble, but instead of that I knew of an old friend of mine who knows how to cure hot burns and cold burns, and so I've been off on a long trip to see the witch doctor, old Mammy-Bammy Big Money.'

"'And did you see her?' says Brother Lion, says he.

"'I most certainly did,' says I, ' and furthermore I laid the whole case before her. I had to travel far and wide to find her, but when I did find her I asked her to tell me what was good for a person who had been scalded by milk-warm water. She asked me three times the name of the person, and three times I told her. Then she lit a pine splinter, blew it out, and watched the smoke scatter. There was something wrong, for she shook her head three times.'

"'What did Mammy-Bammy Big Money say ?'

says Brother Lion, says he. His voice sounded very weak.

"'She said nothing,' says I. 'She watched the smoke scatter, and then she put her hands before her face and rocked from side to side. After that she walked back and forth, and when she sat down again she took off her left slipper, shook out the gravel, and counted it as it fell. Once more she asked me the name of the person who had been scalded .in milk-warm water, and once more I told her.'

"'Wait!' says Brother Lion, says he. 'Do you mean to tell me the water I fell in was only milk-warm?'

"Says I, 'It seemed so to me. I had just washed my face and hands in it.'

"'Well, well, well!' says Brother Lion. 'What else did she say?' says he.

"'I don't like to tell you,' says I; and just about that time Brother Fox walked in.

"'But you must tell me,' says Brother Lion, says he.

"'Well,' says I, 'if I must I will, but I don't like to. When Mammy-Bammy Big Money had counted the white pebbles that fell from her slipper, and asked me the name of the person who was scalded in milk-warm water, she told me that he could be cured by poulticing the burns with the fresh hide of his best friend. I asked her the name of this friend, but she shook her head and said she would call no names. Then she said that your best friend had short ears, a sharp nose, keen eyes, slim legs, and a bushy tail.'

" Brother Lion shut his eyes and pretended to be thinking. I looked at Brother Fox as solemnly as I knew how, and shook my head slowly. Brother Fox got mighty restless. He got up and walked around.

" ' Well, well, well!' says Brother Lion, says he. 'That might mean Brother Wolf, or it might mean Brother Fox.'

" ' I expect it means Brother Wolf,' says Brother Fox.

" ' Why, you don't mean to stand up here and say right before Brother Lion's face and eyes that Brother Wolf is a better friend to him than you are!' says I.

" Brother Fox's mouth fell open and his tongue hung out, and just about that time I made my best bow, and put out for home."

" But did Brother Lion try the remedy ? " Buster John inquired, as Mr. Rabbit paused and began to light his pipe.

"I think Brother Lion caught him and skinned him. It 's a great pity if he did n't. But I 'll not be certain. So many things have happened since then that I disremember about the hide business. But you may be sure Brother Lion was very superstitious. My best opinion is that he tried the cure."

XV.

"THAT is a funny name for a witch," said Buster John, as Rabbit paused and began to nod.

"Which name was that?" inquired Mr. Thimblefinger.

"Why, Mammy-Bammy Big Money," replied Buster John, elevating his voice a little.

"Well, it's very simple," remarked Mr. Thimblefinger. "'Mammy-Bammy' was to catch the ear of the animals, and 'Big-Money' was to attract the attention of the people."

"Dat's so," said Drusilla. "Kaze time you say 'money' folks 'll stop der work an' lissen at you; an' ef you say 'Big-Money' dey'll ax you ter say it agin'."

"It's very curious about money," continued Mr. Thimblefinger. "I don't know whether you ever thought about it much—and I hope you have n't—but it has pestered me a good deal, this thing you call money."

"It's mighty bothersome," assented Mrs. Meadows, "when you are where people use it, and when you have none except what you can beg or borrow. Thank goodness! I'm free from all bother now."

"Yes," said Mr. Thimblefinger, "I don't see that people have much the advantage of the animals when it comes to using money. I've seen grown people work night and day for a few pieces of metal."

"Why, of course!" cried Buster John. "They can take the pieces of metal and buy bread and meat to eat and clothes to wear."

"So much the more wonderful!" remarked Mr. Thimblefinger. "What do the people who have more bread and meat and clothes than they can use want with the pieces of metal?"

"So they may buy something else that they have n't got," said Buster John.

But Mr. Thimblefinger shook his head. He was not satisfied.

"It puts me in mind of a tale I heard once about a poor man who was the richest person in the world."

"But that could n't be, you know," protested Buster John.

"Anyhow, that's the way it seemed to me in the story," replied Mr. Thimblefinger. "But the story is so old-fashioned it would hardly pass muster now. Besides, they tell me that, as there's not enough metal to go round, people have begun to make up their minds that pieces of paper with pictures on them are just as good as the metal, and perhaps better. It's mighty funny to me."

"What was the story?" asked Sweetest Susan. "Please tell us about it."

"Why, yes," remarked Mr. Rabbit, "tell us about it. If calamus root passes current with some of my acquaintances and catnip with others, I see no reason why people should n't play make-believe among themselves, and say that pieces of metal and pieces of paper are worth something. In this business people have a great advantage over us. They can put figures on their pieces of metal and paper and make them worth anything, but with us a joint of calamus root is worth just so much. It has been worth that since the year one, and it will be worth that right on to the end of things. Just so with a twist of catnip. But tell us the story—tell us the story. I may drop off to sleep, but if I do, that will be no sign that the tale is n't interesting."

"Well," said Mr. Thimblefinger, "once upon a time there was a country in which money became very scarce. The people had a great deal, but they hid it in their stockings and in the chinks of the chimneys and in their teapots. The reason of this was that other countries close at hand made their money out of the same kind of metal, and they'd bring their goods in and sell them and carry the money off home with them.

"Of course this helped to make money scarce, and the scarcer it was the more the people clung to it, and this made it still scarcer. Naturally everybody kept an eye out in the hope of finding a supply of this metal."

"What sort of metal was it?" asked Buster John.

"Gold," replied Mr. Thimblefinger.

"Oh!" exclaimed Buster John, in a disappointed tone.

"Yes," continued Mr. Thimblefinger, "nothing in the world but gold. Those who had money held on to it as long as they could, because they did n't know how much scarcer it would be, and those who did n't have any were willing to sell whatever they had for any price in order to get some.

"It was lots worse than playing dolls — lots worse. When children play make-believe with dolls, they soon forget about it; but when grown people begin to play make-believe with money, they never get over it. The wisest men get their heads turned when they begin to think and talk about money. They have forgotten that it was all a make-believe in the beginning."

Here Mr. Rabbit yawned and said: "You 'll have to excuse me if I nod a little here."

"Yes," remarked Mrs. Meadows, "I feel a little sleepy myself, but I 'll try to keep awake for the sake of appearances."

"Don't mind me," said Mr. Thimblefinger, with mock politeness. "Go to sleep if you want to, you two. I won't have to talk so loud.

"Well, in this country I was telling you about, there was a young man who had saved some money by working hard, but he did n't save it fast enough to suit himself. He thought so much about it that he would stop in the middle of his work, and sit and study about it an hour at a time.

"He thought about it so much that he began to dream about it, and one night he dreamed that he got in a boat and went to an island on which there was a mountain of gold that shone and glistened in the sun. He was very unhappy when he woke in the morning and found it was nothing but a dream.

" He did n't go to work that day, but wandered about doing nothing. That night he had the same dream. He had the same dream the next night; and the morning after, the first person he saw was an old man who had stopped to rest on the doorsteps. This old man would have been like other old men but for one thing. His beard was so long that he had to part it in the middle of his chin, pass it under each arm, cross the wisps on his back, and bring them around in front again, where the two ends were tied together with a bow of red ribbon.

" ' How are you, my young friend, and how goes it?' said the old man, smiling pleasantly. 'You look as if you had been having wonderful dreams.'

" ' So I have, gran'sir,' replied the young man.

" ' Well, a dream is n't worth a snap of your finger unless it comes true, and a dream never comes true until you have dreamed it three times.'

"'I have dreamed mine three times, gran'sir, and yet it is impossible that it should come true.'

"'Nonsense! Nothing is impossible. Tell me your dream.'

"So the young man told the old man his dream.

"'The Island of the Mountain of Gold!' exclaimed the old man. 'Why, that is right in my line of travel. I can land you there without any trouble. It is a little out of my way, but not much.'

"'How shall we get there?' the young man asked.

"'On the other side of the town, I have a boat,' replied the old man. 'You are welcome to go with me. It is so seldom that dreams come true that I shall be glad to help this one along as well as I can. Besides, I have long wanted an excuse to visit the Island of the Mountain of Gold. I have passed within sight of it hundreds of times, but have always been too busy to land there.'

"The young man looked at the old man with

astonishment. If he had spoken his thoughts he would have declared the old man to be crazy, but he said nothing. He simply followed after him. The old man led the way across the town to a wharf, where his boat was tied. It was a light little skiff that could be sailed by one man. In this the two embarked.

" The old man managed the sail with one hand and the rudder with the other, and he had hardly made things ready and taken his seat before a light breeze sprang up and filled the sail. The skiff glided along the water so easily that the shore seemed to be receding while the boat stood still. But the breeze grew stronger and stronger, and the sail bore so heavily on the nose of the boat that the foam and spray flew high in the air.

" The sun was bright and the sky was blue, and the dark green water seemed to boil beneath them, so swiftly the light boat sped along. The young man clapped his hands as joyously as a boy, and the old man smiled. Presently he leaned over the side of the boat and pointed to something shining and sparkling in the distance. The young man saw it, too, and turned an inquiring eye upon his companion.

"'That is your mountain of gold,' said the old man.

"'It seems to be very small,' said the other. He ceased to smile, and a frown clouded his face.

"The old man noticed the frown, and shook his head and frowned a little himself, coughing in the muffler that was tied around his neck. But he said : —

"'The mountain of gold is more than twenty miles away.'

"'How far have we come?'

"'Some hundred and odd miles.'

"The young man seemed to be very much surprised, but he said nothing. He leaned so far over the side of the boat to watch the mountain of gold that he was in danger of falling out. The old man kept an eye on him, but did not lift a finger to warn him.

"In due time they came to the island, if it could be called an island. It seemed to be a barren rock that had lifted itself out of the sea to show the mountain of gold. The mountain was only a hill, but it was a pretty high one, considering it was of solid gold."

"Sure enough gold?" asked Sweetest Susan.

"Pure gold," answered Mr. Thimblefinger. "The old man landed his skiff at a convenient place, and the two got out and went to the mountain, or hill, of gold that rose shining in the middle of the small island. The actions of the young man showed that he considered himself the proprietor of both island and mountain. He broke off a chunk of gold as big as your fist, weighed it in his hand, and would have given it to the old man, but the latter shook his head.

"'You refuse it?' cried the other. 'If it is not enough I'll give you as much more.'

"'No,' replied the old man. 'Keep it for yourself. You owe me nothing. I could have carried away tons of the stuff long before I saw you, but I had no use for it. You are welcome to as much as you can take away with you.'

"'As much as I can take away!' exclaimed the other. 'I shall take it all.'

"'But how?'

"'It is mine! I am rich. I will buy me a ship.' He walked back and forth, rubbing his hands together.

"'Then you have no further need of me?' said the old man.

" 'Not now — not now,' replied the other with a grand air. 'You won't accept pay for your services, and I can do no more than thank you.'

" The old man bowed politely, got in his skiff, and sailed away. The other continued to walk about the island and rub his hands together, and make his plans. He was now the richest man in the world. He could buy kings and princes and empires. He had enough gold to buy all the ships on the sea and to control all the trade on the land. He was great. He was powerful.

" All these thoughts passed through his mind and he was very happy. The sun looked at the young man a long time, and then went to bed in the sea. Two little gray lizards looked at him until the sun went down, and then they crawled back in their holes. A big black bird sailed round and round and watched him until nearly dark, and then sailed away.

" When night came the young man found the air damp and chilly, but he knew he was rich, and so he laughed at the cold. He crept close under his mountain of gold, and, after a long time, went to sleep. In the morning he awoke and found that nobody had taken away his precious moun-

HE WAS SO WEAK THAT HE COULDN'T GET UP

tain of gold during the night. The sun rose to keep him company, the two gray lizards crept out of their holes and looked at him, and the big black bird sailed round and round overhead.

"The day passed, and then another and another. The young man was hungry and thirsty, but he was rich. The night winds chilled him, but he was rich. The midday sun scorched him, but he was the richest man in the world. Every night, no matter how hungry or weak he was, he crept upon the side of the mountain, and stretched himself out, and tried to hug it to his bosom. He knew that if he was hungry, it was n't because he was poor, and if he died, he knew he would die rich. So there he was."

"What then?" asked Buster John, as Mr. Thimblefinger paused to look at his watch.

"Well, I 'll tell you," continued Mr. Thimblefinger, holding the watch to his ear. "One fine morning this rich young man was so weak that he could n't get up. He tried to, but his foot slipped, and he rolled to the foot of the mountain of gold and lay there. He lay there so long and so quietly that the two gray lizards crept close to him to see what was the matter. He moved one of his fingers, and they darted back to their holes.

"The rich young man lay so still that the big black bird, sailing overhead, came nearer and nearer, and finally alighted at a respectful distance from the rich young man. The two gray lizards came out again, and crawled cautiously toward the rich young man. The big black bird craned his neck and looked, and then went a little closer. A sudden gust of wind caused the rich young man's coat to flap. The gray lizards scrambled towards their holes, and the big black bird jumped up in the air and flew off a little way.

"But presently they all came back, bird and lizards, and this time they went still closer to the rich young man. The big black bird went so close that there is no telling what he would have done next, but just then the old man came running towards them. He had untied the two ends of his beard, and was waving them in the air as if they were flags. The big black bird flew away very angry, and the gray lizards ran over each other trying to get to their holes.

"The old man tied up his beard again, took up

the rich young man on his shoulder, and carried him to the boat. Once there he gave the rich young man some wine. This revived him, and in a little while he was able to eat. But he had no opportunity to talk. The wind whirled the boat through the water, and in a few hours it had arrived at the young man's town.

"He went home, and soon recovered in more ways than one. He found his strength again, and lost his appetite for riches. But he worked hard, saved all he could, and was soon prosperous; but he never remembered without a shiver the time that he was the richest man in the world."

XVI.

AN OLD-FASHIONED FUSS.

"I DON'T blame 'im fer shiverin'," said Drusilla; "but, I let you know, here's what would n't shiver none ef she had dat ar big pile er gol' what de man had. I'd 'a' cotch me some fish; I'd 'a' gobbled up dem lizards, yit!"

"Well," remarked Mr. Rabbit, "I expect money is a pretty big thing. I've heard a heap of talk about it, and I've known some big fusses to grow out of it. And yet money does n't cause all the fusses — oh, no! not by a long jump. I once heard of a fuss that happened long before there was any money, and the curious part about it was that nobody knew what the fuss grew out of."

"What fuss was that?" asked Buster John, who thought that perhaps there might be a story in it.

"Why, it was the quarrel between the Monkeys and the Dogs. My great-grandfather knew all about the facts, and I 've heard him talk it over many a time when he was sitting in the kitchen corner chewing his quid. I 've often heard him wonder, between naps, what caused the dispute."

"It seems to me I 've heard something about it," remarked Mrs. Meadows in an encouraging tone.

"Oh, yes!" exclaimed Mr. Rabbit. "It was notorious in our young days. I reckon it has been settled long before this; anyhow, I hope so."

"What did your great-grandfather say about it?" inquired Buster John.

"If I were to tell you all he said," responded Mr. Rabbit, shaking his head slowly, "you 'd have to sit here with me for a fortnight, and of course you would n't like to do that. So I 'll just up and tell you about it in my own way. I may not get it exactly right, but I 'll be bound I won't get it far wrong, for I have nothing else in the round world to do but to sit here and think about old times.

"As well as I can remember, the way of it was about this : Away back yonder, in the times before everybody had got to be so busy trying to get the best of each other, a coolness sprang up between the Monkeys and the Dogs. Nobody knew the right of it, because nobody paid any attention to it along at first. But after awhile it got so that every time a Dog would meet a Monkey in the road, the Monkey would get up in a tree and laugh at him, and then the Dog would stop and scratch up the dirt with all four of his feet and growl."

"Oh, I 've seen them do that way," said Sweetest Susan, laughing.

"Yes," replied Mr. Rabbit, with a more solemn air than ever. "They have never got out of the habit of that kind of caper from that day to this. Well, the coolness grew into a dispute, and the dispute into a quarrel, and so there it was. The Monkeys would make faces and squeal at the Dogs, and the Dogs would show their teeth and growl at the Monkeys. It went from bad to worse, and after awhile, the Dogs would chase the Monkeys wherever they saw them, and the Monkeys would swing down from the hanging limbs and give the tails of the Dogs some terrible twists.

"Before that time the Monkeys had been living on the ground just like everybody else lived,

THE MONKEYS WOULD MAKE FACES AND SQUEAL AT THE
DOGS

but the Dogs had such sharp teeth and such nimble feet that the Monkeys had to take to the trees and saplings. At first they could n't get about in the trees as they do now. Sometimes they 'd miss their footing, or lose their grip, and down they 'd come right into the red jaws of the Dogs.

"Now this was n't pleasant at all. Even when the Monkeys did n't fall, the ants and crawling bugs would get on them, and the dead limbs of the trees would fall and hurt them, and the wind would blow them about, and the heavy rains would fall and wet them.

"About that time the Monkeys were the most miserable creatures in the world. They were so miserable that, finally, the Head Monkey made up his mind to go and see the Wise Man who used to settle all disputes as far as he could. So the Head Monkey set out on his journey, and traveled till he came to the Wise Man's house.

"He got on the gatepost, and looked all around, to see if there was a Dog anywhere in sight. Seeing none, he went to the front door and knocked. The Wise Man came out. He was very old. He had a beard as long as Brother

Billy Goat's, and as gray, but he was very nice and kind. The Head Monkey told his story all the way through, and the Wise Man sat and listened to every word. When he had heard it all, he shut his eyes and studied the matter over, and then he said : —

" ' Only fools get up fusses that they can't settle. I 'll give you a fool's remedy to settle a fool's fuss. Go back to your own country and fetch me a bunch of the hair of a Brindle Dog. Then I 'll show you a cheap and an easy way to get rid of the whole tribe of Dogs. But be sure that you make no mistake. I must have the hair of a Brindle Dog—just that and nothing else. Then I can show you how to get rid of all the Dogs. But if you make any mistake, you will ruin the whole tribe of Monkeys.'

" The Head Monkey scratched himself on the side, quick like. Says he, ' Oh, I 'll make no mistake. Don't worry about me. The first time the Dogs have a burying I 'll get on a swinging limb, and when a Brindle Dog comes along I 'll reach down and pull a bunch of hair out of his hide, and by the time he gets through howling I 'll be on my journey back.'

" The Wise Man ran his fingers through his beard, and laughed to himself. Says he, ' Very well, my young friend, but you had best be careful. A Dog of any kind will bear watching, but especially a Brindle Dog.'

" The Head Monkey made no answer. He simply grinned, and started back home. Now, it happened that after his journey was over, the Dogs had no burying for a long time. They seemed to be in better health than ever. Some traveling doctor had come along and told them that whenever they felt out of sorts they must go out in the fields and hunt for a particular kind of grass. When they found it they were to eat twenty-seven blades of it, and then go on about their business. You may not believe this," said Mr. Rabbit, pausing in the midst of his story, " but if you will watch the Dogs right close, you will find that to this day they 'll go out and eat grass whenever they are ailing. They don't chew it. They just bite off a great long sprig of it, and wallop it around their tongues and swallow it whole. I don't know how they do it, but I 'm telling you the plain facts.

" Well, as I was saying, it was a long time

after the Head Monkey got home before the Dogs had a burying, and when they did have one it happened that there was no Brindle Dog in the procession. The rest of the Monkeys were all waiting to see what the Head Monkey was going to do, and so they forgot to bother the Dogs. When the Dogs saw that the Monkeys were quiet, they kept quiet themselves, and there was no trouble between them for a long time. Seeing that the Dogs were no longer snapping and snarling at them, some of the older Monkeys began to travel on the ground again, but the younger ones stayed in the trees where they were born.

"The Head Monkey was mighty restless. Sometimes he 'd stay in the trees, and then again he 'd travel on the ground, but wherever he was he always kept his eye out for a Brindle Dog. Finally, one day, when he was traveling on the ground, he heard a noise up the road, and when he turned around he saw a big Brindle Dog coming towards him. He thought to himself that now was his time or never; so he got behind a bush and waited for the Brindle Dog to come up.

" He did n't have long to wait, for the Brindle Dog was going in a swinging trot. When he came by the bush, the Head Monkey rushed out and tried to pull a bunch of hair from the Brindle Dog's hide. But he rushed too far. The Brindle Dog shied, as old Mr. Horse used to do when he saw a bunch of shucks in the road. He shied so quick, and he shied so far, that the Head Monkey fell short with his arm, and was carried too far by his legs. As the Brindle Dog shied, he turned and saw what it was, and then he made a rush for the Head Monkey. There was no tree near, and no way for the Head Monkey to escape. The Brindle Dog grabbed him and made short work of him. There was considerable of a fight, for the Head Monkey was strong in his arms and quick on his feet. But the Brindle Dog had a long jaw and a strong one. He grabbed the Head Monkey between shoulder and ham, and shook him up as you have seen people shake a sifter. He just held on and shook, and when he turned loose he 'd shut his teeth down in a new place, so that when the rippit was over, it seemed as if there was n't a whole bone in the Head Monkey's hide. But quick done is quick over : and after the Brindle Dog had done all the shaking that the case called for, he dropped the Head Monkey and went on about his business; but he had some bites and scratches on his hide, and as he trotted off he shook his ears, for one of them had been split mighty nigh in two by the Head Monkey.

"Well, after the Brindle Dog had trotted off, the Head Monkey rose from the ground and began to feel of himself. He was afraid that he had been torn in two and scattered all over the road, but when he found that he had his legs and his arms and his head and his body, he began to be more cheerful. He found he could walk. And then he found he could use his hands, and then he strutted around, and said to himself that he had whipped the fight. He was badly bruised and pretty sore, but he was not too sore to strut, and so he walked up and down the road and made his brags that he had compelled the Brindle Dog to take to his heels.

"Then he happened to think what he had come for, and he hunted all about in the road to see if he could find a bunch of the Brindle Dog's hair. There was a good deal of hair scattered around, and in a little while the Head Monkey had gathered up a handful. He picked it over and sorted it out, and wrapped it up in a poplar leaf. Then he went home to his family and rested a day or two, for he was pretty badly bruised. And he told a big tale of how he had met the great Brindle Dog in the road, and had fanned him out in a fair fight. His children listened with all their ears, and then they jumped from limb to limb and told all the neighbors' children that their pa was the biggest and the best of all the Monkeys.

"This went on for some time, and finally the Head Monkey felt well enough to visit the Wise Man. So he started on the journey, and after awhile he got there. He climbed the gatepost again, and looked all around to see if there was a Brindle Dog in sight. Seeing none, he went to the door and knocked, and the Wise Man came out.

"'Good-morning,' says the Wise Man. 'I hope you are well.'

"'Tolerably well, I thank you,' says the Head Monkey. 'And I 've come agreeable to promise to bring you a bunch of the hair of a Brindle Dog.'

"With that he unrolled the poplar leaf, and

showed the Wise Man the hair he had picked up in the road. The Wise Man took the bunch of hair and turned it over in his hand, and looked at it. Then he looked at the Head Monkey.

"'What is this?' says he.

"'A bunch of hair from a Brindle Dog,' says the Head Monkey.

"The Wise Man shook his head. Says he, 'It may be, but it does n't look like the samples I have seen. Are you sure about it?' says he.

"'As sure as I am standing here,' says the Head Monkey.

"Says the Wise Man, 'It's none of my business. I just wanted to be certain about it, because if there's any Monkey hair in it, everything will go wrong. The whole tribe of Monkeys will be ruined. They will have to leave this country and the Dogs will stay here. Did you have any trouble in getting this hair?' says he.

"'Well,' says the Head Monkey, 'there was a dispute, nothing serious.'

"'How long did the dispute last?' says the Wise Man.

"'No longer than I could reach out and get the hair,' says the Head Monkey.

" 'That's funny,' says the Wise Man. 'When the Brindle Dog gets into a dispute, he usually shows his teeth.'

" 'Oh, he showed his teeth, and he had more than I thought,' says the Head Monkey.

" 'But are you sure this hair came out of the hide of a Brindle Dog ?' says the Wise Man.

" Says the Head Monkey, 'As sure as I 'm standing here. I pulled it out with my own hands.'

" Says the Wise Man, 'It looks to me as if there were some other kind of hair in this bunch. Did you have any trouble in getting it ?' says he.

" 'Well,' says the Head Monkey, 'we had a little dispute.'

" Says the Wise Man, 'Was that all ?'

" 'Well,' says the Head Monkey, scratching himself, ' we passed a few licks.'

" ' How was that ?' says the Wise Man.

" ' Well,' says the Head Monkey, ' he growled and I squealed, and then he bit and I scratched.'

" 'I see,' says the Wise Man. ' What else ?'

" ' Well, to tell you the truth,' says the Head Monkey, 'there was right smart of a scuffle.'

" 'Aha !' says the Wise Man. 'A scuffle !'

"'Yes,' says the Head Monkey, 'and worse than that. There was a regular knock-down-and-drag-out fight,' says he.

"'I see,' says the Wise Man. 'You have brought me some of your own hair instead of the Brindle Dog's hair, and now you and your whole tribe will have to leave this country and cross the ocean; and when you get into the new country, you will have to live in the trees to keep the four-footed animals from destroying you.'

"And so it happened," continued Mr. Rabbit. "Since that time, there have been no Monkeys in this country. They had to cross the big water, and when they got over there they had to live in the trees; and I expect they are living that way yet — at least, they were at last accounts."

XVII.

THE RABBIT AND THE MOON.

"I RECKON that's so about the Monkeys," remarked Mrs. Meadows. "They used to be in the country next door, and now they are no longer there."

"Yes," said Mr. Rabbit; "it's just like I tell you: they were there once, but now they are not there any more. But in the world next door everybody has his ups and downs, especially his downs. I've heard my great-grandfather tell many a time how our family used to live close to the Moon. So I don't make any brags about the way the Monkeys had to take to the bushes. I remember about my own family, and then I feel like hanging my head down and saying nothing. It is a very funny feeling, too. When I think we used to live close to the Moon, and that we now live on the ground and have to crawl there like snails, I sometimes feel like crying; and I tell you right now if I was to begin to boohoo, you'd be astonished."

Buster John and Sweetest Susan looked very serious, but Drusilla showed a desire to laugh.

"You say you used to live close to the Moon?" asked Buster John, with more curiosity than usual.

"Why, certainly," replied Mr. Rabbit. "I don't say that I did, but I'm certain that my family did. I've heard my great-grandfather tell about it a hundred times. I've heard that it was a better country up there than it is where you live, even better than it is down here, — a good deal more fun and fiddling, and not half so much looking around for something to eat. That is the great trouble. If we did n't have to scuffle around and get something to eat, we'd be lots better off.

"It's mighty funny. If you let well enough alone, you are all right; but the minute you try to better it, everything goes wrong."

"Dat wuz de way wid ol' man Adam," remarked Drusilla.

"Why, of course," said Mr. Rabbit, "and it was the way with all the Rabbits and everybody and everything else."

"But how did they live up there by the

Moon?" asked Sweetest Susan. "How did they keep from falling off?"

Mr. Rabbit scratched his head a little before replying. "Well," said he, after awhile, "they got along just as we do down here,—heads up and feet down. But one time, as I 've heard my great-grandfather say, the Moon got into a sort of fidget, and was mighty restless for quite a while. At last, one of our family, the oldest of all, made bold to look over the fence and ask the Moon what the trouble was. He noticed, too, that the Moon had shrunk considerably, and seemed to be in a very bad way. It could hardly hold up its head.

"But the Moon managed to look up when it heard the fuss at the fence, and, in a very shaky voice, told the oldest of all the Rabbits howdy.

"'What is the trouble?' says the oldest Rabbit. Says he, 'Can I do anything to help you?'

"'I 'm afraid not,' says the Moon. 'You are not nimble enough.'

"'Maybe I 'm nimbler than you think,' says the oldest Rabbit.

"'Well,' says the Moon, 'I 'll tell you what the trouble is. I want to get a message to Mr.

Man, who lives in the world down yonder. I 've
been shining on him at night, and I 've caught a
bad cold by being out after dark. My health is
breaking down, and if I don't put out my lights
for a while and take a rest, I 'll have to go
out altogether. Now, it 's like this: I 've been
shining for Mr. Man so long that if I don't send
him some word he 'll think something serious has
happened. I must take a rest, but I want to
send him a message, telling him that I won't be
gone long.'

" ' Well,' says the oldest Rabbit, ' I don't mind
going, if you 'll show me the way and tell me
what to say.'

"So the Moon pointed out the way, and showed
him how to put his fingers in his ears and hold
his breath when he took the long jump. Then it
gave him this message:—

   ' *I am growing weak to gather strength:*

   I go into the shadows to gather light.'

" The oldest Rabbit said this message over to
himself many times, and then he got ready for
the journey. Everything went well until he came
to the long jump. But he braced himself, and
shut his eyes, and put his fingers in his ears, and

"WHAT IS THE TROUBLE?" SAYS THE OLDEST RABBIT

held his breath. Now, the jump was a long one, sure enough. It was so long that the oldest Rabbit opened one eye, and then he got the notion that he was falling instead of jumping, and he opened both eyes so wide that they have been that way ever since. This scared him terribly, and by the time he landed on the world he had forgotten what he came for. He was n't hurt a bit, but he was badly scared.

" He sat on the ground and tried to remember, and then he got up and walked about. Finally, he looked up and saw the Moon winking one eye at him. Then he thought about the message, and he ran off to Mr. Man's house, and knocked at the door. Mr. Man had gone to bed, but he got up and opened the door, and asked what was wanted.

" ' Well,' says the oldest Rabbit, ' I 've just come from the Moon with a message for you.'

" ' What is it?' says Mr. Man.

" ' The Moon told me to tell you this : —

' *I 'm growing weak and have no strength :*

I 'm going off where the shadows are dark.'

" Mr. Man scratched his head. He could n't make the message out. Then he said, ' Take this message back : —

    ' Seldom seen and soon forgot :
    When a Moon dies her feet get cold.'

"The oldest Rabbit bowed politely and started back home. He came to the Jumping-Off Place, and then he took the long jump. He was soon at home, and went at once to the Moon's house, and gave the message that Mr. Man had sent. This made the Moon very mad. It declared that the oldest Rabbit had carried the wrong message. Then it grabbed the shovel and struck him in the face. This made the oldest Rabbit very mad, and he jumped at the Moon and used his claws. The fight was a hard one, and you can see the marks of it to this day. All the Rabbits have their upper lips split, and the Moon still has the marks on its face where the oldest Rabbit 'clawed it.

"The way of it was this," continued Mr. Rabbit, seeing that the children had hardly caught the drift of the story: "the Moon had been shining constantly for many years, and was growing weak. It wanted to take a rest, and it was afraid Mr. Man would get scared when he failed to see it at night. Since that time the Moon has been taking a rest about every two weeks. At least it used to be that way. I never bother about it now."

XVIII.

WHY THE BEAR IS A WRESTLER.

"Well," said Mr. Rabbit, after a pause, "what about the story? Was there any moral to it?"

"None at all," replied Mrs. Meadows. "It was just an old-time tale."

"Now, I'm truly glad to hear you say so," cried Mr. Rabbit, appearing to be very much pleased. "It's as good as taking a nap." He winked gravely at Buster John, and then proceeded to refill his pipe.

"I thought it was a pretty good story," said Buster John. "It turned out to be a story so quick that it was all over with before I knew it was a story."

"Well," replied Mr. Rabbit, "I had to tell it mighty quick. Suppose I had stopped to light my pipe and left my own kin dangling between the Moon and the World! I knew in reason it would never do, and so I rattled away almost as fast as the oldest Rabbit jumped.   It was a long story quickly told of a long journey quickly made."

Mr. Rabbit seemed to be in better humor than ever.   He leaned back, and patted the ground softly with one foot.

" Speaking of journeys," he said, after awhile, " makes me think about how Brother Bear started out in the world.   But what am I doing?" he cried.   " I don't want to do all the talking.   I don't have any chance to sleep unless somebody else is telling a story."

" Now, please tell us the story," pleaded Sweetest Susan.

" I 'll have to," replied Mr. Rabbit, " since I 've got it started.   Well, one time when Brother Bear was young, the time came for him to scratch around and scuffle for himself.   He had already learned how to grabble for sweet potatoes, how to tote an armful of roasting ears, and how to shut his eyes and rob a bee-tree, and so his daddy thought it was about time for him to go off and earn his own living.   Brother Bear said he was more than willing, and when he came to tell his folks good-by, his daddy gave him seven pieces of honey-in-the-comb, saying : —

" 'This is all I have to give you, but it's enough. Whoever eats this honey with you will have to wrestle with you seven years or give you everything he owns.'

" So Brother Bear put his seven pieces of honey-in-the-comb in a bag, slung the bag over his back, and went shuffling down the big road. He traveled all that day, and camped out in the woods at night. The next morning, just as he was about to eat breakfast, he heard a rustling in the bushes, and presently Brother Tiger came slipping and sliding along, hunting for his break-fast. Brother Bear howdied, and Brother Tiger said he was only tolerable — not as peart as he might be, and yet pearter than he had been. Then Brother Tiger sat and watched Brother Bear take out a piece of his honey-in-the-comb, and the sight made his mouth water. Brother Bear noticed this, and he says, says he : —

" 'I wish you mighty well, Brother Tiger, and I'd like to ask you to have some of my break-fast, for I have more than a plenty for two. But the trouble is, that whoever eats any of this honey-in-the-comb will have to wrestle with me seven years or give me all his belongings.'

"'Don't let that bother you,' says Brother Tiger, says he. 'I'm a pretty good wrestler myself, and I don't mind trying my hand with you after I've tasted your honey-in-the-comb.'

"But Brother Bear hemmed and hawed, and acted so that Brother Tiger thought he was either afraid to wrestle or mighty stingy with his honey-in-the-comb. He thought so, and he said so, and this put Brother Bear on his mettle. So he says, says he: —

"'Well, Brother Tiger, come and get a piece of my honey-in-the-comb. I'm more than glad to give it to you, and sorry, too, because, as sure as you eat it, you'll be put under a spell, and you'll be obliged to wrestle with me seven long years or give me all your belongings.'

"Brother Tiger grinned from ear to ear. Says he, 'If I don't have to wrestle before I get the honey-in-the-comb, it will be all right. Just let me get my fill of that, and I'll wrestle with you seven times seven years. I'll promise to make you tired of wrestling.'

"'So be it,' says Brother Bear. 'Come and get the honey-in-the-comb, and take all you want, for I won't need any after I've wrestled with you a time or two,' says he.

"Brother Tiger went up and tasted the honey-in-the-comb, and it was so good that he smacked his lips and asked for more. Brother Bear gave him some. After both had eat as much as they wanted, Brother Tiger took a notion to go home, but something held him back. The spell was working. But finally he pulled himself together, and said he believed he'd go home and see his old woman.

"But Brother Bear chuckled to himself. Says he, 'Now that you've gobbled up my honey-in-the-comb, you don't want to wrestle. You can't help yourself. When I say wrestle, you'll have to wrestle. You can go home now, but to-morrow, bright and early, I'll knock at your door, and you'll have to come out and wrestle.'

"Says Brother Tiger, says he, 'I'll be more than glad to accommodate you. Just knock at the door any hour after daybreak, and you'll find me on hand.'

"Says Brother Bear, 'I'll do so, I'll do so. Just remember your spoken word, Brother Tiger!'

"Brother Tiger started home, but before he had gone very far he began to feel mighty queer.

He had a buzzing noise in his head and a creepy, crawly feeling on his hide. He began to get scared. Once he thought the honey had poisoned him, but he was n't sick. He never felt better in his life. He wanted to jump and run, and I believe the tale does say that he capered around a time or two. But every time he 'd start home he 'd have that buzzing sound in his head and that creepy, crawly feeling in his hide.

"So, by and by, he thought he would turn back and see what Brother Bear thought about it. No sooner said than done. He went back at a hand gallop, and found Brother Bear curled up at the foot of a tree fast asleep. The honey had made him feel so good that he concluded to enjoy himself by taking another nap. But he got up brisk enough when he heard Brother Tiger calling him, and by the time he had rubbed his eyes once or twice, and gaped and stretched himself, he was as wide awake as ever.

"Says he, 'I knew you 'd come back, Brother Tiger, and so I just waited for you; and while I was waiting I ups and drops off to sleep. But anyhow and anyway, here you are, and there 's no harm done.'

"Says Brother Tiger, says he, 'I just came back to ask you about the queer feeling I have.'

"Says Brother Bear, 'That's easy enough. You just wanted to wrestle, and so you had to come back. I have the feeling most all the time when I'm not sleeping or eating. It's a sort of zooning sound in the ears, and a sort of ticklish feeling on the hide. Well, there is n't anything the matter at all. You just want to wrestle, and as the feeling is new to you, you did n't know what it was.'

"Says Brother Tiger, 'I believe you are right, Brother Bear; I believe that's the whole trouble.'

"'Well,' says Brother Bear, 'I'll try you one round, just to loosen up my hide and put me in traveling trim. I'll not wrestle with you very hard, because you are not used to it, and it's too soon to get down to business with you. I told you about it when you wanted to eat the honey, but you would eat it, and now you'll have to wrestle with me, off and on, first and last, for seven long years; and if you don't, you'll have to give me your house and all your belongings.'

"So they took off their coats and made ready to wrestle. 'As you are not used to these capers,' says Brother Bear, 'I 'll give you all-under holt, and promise not to use the in-turn, the ham-twist, or the knee-lock.'

"Now, Brother Tiger did n't know whether Brother Bear was talking Latin or Chinese, but he said nothing: he just stood up and grabbed Brother Bear around the waist, or where the waist ought to be.

"'When you are ready,' says Brother Bear, 'just give the word.'

"'Well,' says Brother Tiger, 'I reckon I 'm as ready now as I ever will be.'

"With that Brother Bear hugged Brother Tiger pretty tight, whirled around with him a time or two, fell on him, and then cuffed him, first on one ear and then on the other. It was all done so quick that Brother Tiger did n't have time to say don't. He got up and felt of his ribs to see if they were still whole, and then he rubbed the side of his head where Brother Bear had cuffed him. It had already begun to swell. His breeches were badly ripped, and he was sore all over.

"Says he, 'And so this is what you call wrestling — this is what I was itching for, is it?'

HE RUBBED THE SIDE OF HIS HEAD

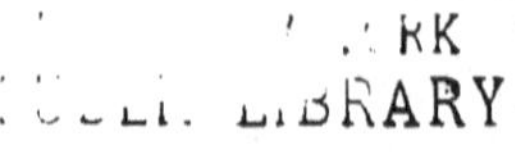

" ' Oh, no ! ' says Brother Bear. ' It would n't do to call that wrestling. That was only playing. I was just showing you the first few capers : you can't wrestle until you learn how. I 'll drop by your house to-morrow morning, bright and early, and give you another whirl.'

" Brother Tiger looked mighty solemn, but he did n't say anything. He ambled off home as well as he could in his condition, and got his old woman to mend his breeches. She wanted to know who he had been fighting with, but he told her he had just been playing with Brother Bear. She laughed, and said that when he had played that way a few more times there would n't be enough of him left, neither breeches, body, nor bones, to sew up in a bag.

" Well, the next morning, bright and early, Brother Bear rapped at Brother Tiger's door, and told him to come out and take some exercise before breakfast. Brother Tiger did n't like this invitation at all. He said he wanted to sleep a little longer ; but Brother Bear sent in word that the night was made for sleeping, while the day was made for work and play. Now, it so happened that the honey which Brother Tiger had ate had put a spell on him, and when Brother Bear asked him out to wrestle he had to come. He pulled on his clothes with no good heart, for he was still very sore, and came limping out, trying to put a good face on the affair. Brother Bear laughed, and told Brother Tiger howdy, but Brother Tiger did n't make much of a reply.

"So Brother Bear says, says he, 'I hope you are not begrudging your bargain, Brother Tiger, but you made it yourself, and at no invitation of mine. I had the seven pieces of honey-in-the-comb, and you had the bad taste in the mouth. I told you how it would be, but you would have the honey, and now you 'll have to stand to your bargain: you can't help yourself now. I told you the plain truth about it, but you would n't believe it. You 'll find out the truth before you get the taste of that honey out of your mouth.'

"Then they made a few passes at each other; but Brother Bear finally grabbed Brother Tiger around his striped waist, squeezed the breath out of him, dashed him on the ground, cuffed his ears, and then stood there on his hind legs, waiting to see what Brother Tiger was going to do. But Brother Tiger did n't want any more wrestling for that day. He went into the house and washed his face and hands, and sat down and licked his bruises the best he could.

"But the next morning he had to come out and wrestle again, and this happened until he was so weak he could hardly walk. His hide was split, his ears were swollen, and every stripe on his long body was crossed by a scar. Wrestling was fine fun for Brother Bear, who was used to it, but it was no fun for Brother Tiger, who did n't know how. Every time he wrestled he got new bruises, and his head swelled until he could hardly get in the door of his house without backing his ears.

"Finally, one day he told Brother Bear candidly that he would rather give up his house and lot than to be tossed around and cuffed at that rate. Brother Bear said that he would rather wrestle and have a jolly time than to take Brother Tiger's house; but Brother Tiger would n't hear to that. He said he could n't stay in that part of the country and hear the talk of the neighbors. They would pester him mighty near to death on the week days, and fairly kill him out on Sunday, when they had nothing to do but sit around and gossip.

"So Brother Tiger moved out, and Brother Bear moved in ; and it has come to pass that Brother Tiger won't stay in the same country with Brother Bear for fear that he will have to do some more wrestling."

XIX.

THE SHOEMAKER WHO MADE BUT ONE SHOE.

"Now, I 'll tell you honestly," said Little Mr. Thimblefinger, popping out from under Mr. Rabbit's big arm-chair, "I don't like such stories. They give me the all-overs. I expect maybe it 's because they are true."

"No doubt that 's the trouble with them," remarked Mr. Rabbit in a tone unusually solemn. "You don't think that at my time of life my tongue is nimble enough for me to sit here and make up stories to suit the hour and the company? By the bye," he continued, turning around so as to catch Little Mr. Thimblefinger's eye, "what stories were you talking about?"

"Well, to tell you the truth, I was fast asleep, for the most part, but I distinctly remember something about Moons and Monkeys. When I heard that, I just went off to sleep in spite of myself."

"There 's no accounting for tastes," said Mr.

Rabbit. "There are some tales that put me to sleep, and I have no complaint to make when anybody begins to doze over them that I tell."

"Oh, you tell 'em well enough," Little Mr. Thimblefinger declared. "If anything, you make them better than they ought to be. You lift your ears at the right place, and pat your foot when the time comes. I don't know what more could be asked in telling a story."

"So far so good," remarked Mrs. Meadows, who had thus far said nothing. "Suppose you whirl in and tell us the kind of tale that you really admire."

"That's easier said than done," replied Little Mr. Thimblefinger, fidgeting about a little. "You have to take the tales as they come. Sometimes one will pop into your head in spite of yourself. You remember it just because you did n't like it when you first heard it."

"Tell us one, anyway, just to pass away the time," said Sweetest Susan.

"If I tell you one," Little Mr. Thimblefinger replied, "I 'll not promise it will be one that I like. That would be promising too much. But the talk about the Moon, that I heard before I dozed off just now, reminded me of a tale I heard when I was a good deal smaller than I am now.

"Once upon a time there was a man who had two sons. They were twins, but they were just as different from each other as they could possibly be. One was dark, and the other was light complected. One was slim, and the other was fat. One was good, and the other was what people call bad. He was lazy, and full of fun and mischief. They grew up that way until they were nineteen or twenty years old. The good boy would work hard every day, or pretend to work hard, and then he 'd go back home and tell his mother and father that his brother had n't done a stroke of work. Of course, this made the old people feel very queer. The mother felt sorrowful, and the father felt angry. This went on, until finally, one day, the father became so angry that he concluded to take his bad son into some foreign country, and bind him out to some person who could make him work and cure him of his mischievousness. In those days people sometimes bound out their children to learn trades and good manners and things of that sort."

"I wish dey 'd do it now," exclaimed Drusilla.

" Kaze den I would n't hafter be playin' nuss, an' be gwine in all kind er quare places whar you dunner when ner whar you kin git out."

"Stuff!" cried Buster John. "Why don't you be quiet and listen to the story?"

" It go long too slow fer ter suit me," said Drusilla in a grumbling tone.

" Well," remarked Mr. Thimblefinger, turning to Buster John, "you 've come mighty close to telling a part of the tale I had in my mind."

" I don't see how," replied Buster John with some surprise.

" You said ' stuff ! ' " responded Mr. Thimblefinger, "and that 's a part of my story. If you listen, you 'll soon find out. As I was saying, people in old times bound out their sons to some good man, who taught them a good trade or something of that kind. Well, this man that I was telling you about took his bad son off to a foreign country, and tried to find some one to bind him out to. They traveled many days and nights. They went over mountains and passed through valleys. They crossed plains, and they went through the wild woods.

" Now, the man who was taking his son into a

foreign country was getting old, and the farther they walked, the more tired he grew. At last, one day, when they were going through the big woods, he sat down to rest near a tall poplar-tree, and, turning to his son, said angrily : —

"'Stuff! you are not worth all this trouble. But for you I 'd be at home now, enjoying myself and smoking my pipe.'

"The son, who was used to these outbreaks, made no reply, but stretched himself out on the dead leaves that littered the ground. He had hardly done so when there was a tremendous noise in the woods, and then both father and son saw rushing toward them an old man with a long beard, followed by a small army of fierce-looking dwarfs armed with clubs and knives and pikes. They rushed up and surrounded the father and son.

"'Which of you called my name and abused me?' cried the old man with the long beard.

"'Not I,' said the bad son.

"'Not I,' said the father. 'I am sure I never saw you or heard of you before.'

"This made the old man more furious than ever. He fairly trembled with rage. 'Did n't I hear one of you say, " Stuff! but for you I 'd be at home now enjoying myself, and smoking my pipe?" '

" ' I did say something like that,' replied the father in great astonishment.

" ' How dare you?' cried the old man, beside himself with rage. ' How did I ever harm you? Seize him!' he said to his army of dwarfs. ' Seize him, and bind him hard and fast! I 'll show him whether he can come into my kingdom and abuse me!'

" The father was speechless with astonishment, and made no attempt to prevent the dwarfs from seizing and binding him. They had him tied hard and fast before he could say a word, even if he had had a word to say. But by this time the son had risen to his feet.

" ' Wait!' he cried, ' let 's see what the trouble is! Who are you?' he inquired, turning to the old man with the long beard.

" ' My name is Stuff,' he replied, ' and I am king of this country which you are passing through. I 'm not going to allow any one to abuse me in my own kingdom. You may go free, but mind you go straight back the way you came.'

"The son thought the matter over a little while, and then turned on his heel and went back the way he had come, and, as he walked, he whistled all the lively tunes he could think of. For a time he was glad that his father was no longer with him to quarrel and complain; but finally he grew lonely, and then he began to think how his father had raised him up from a little child. The more he thought about this, the sorrier he was that he had given his father any trouble. He sat down on a log by the side of the road and thought it all over, and presently he began to cry.

"While he was sitting there with his head between his hands, crying over the fate of his father, a queer-looking little man came jogging along the road. He had bushy hair and a beard that grew all over his face, except right around his eyes and lips and the tip-end of his nose. His beard was not long, but it was very thick, and it stood out around his face like the spokes in a buggy-wheel. He seemed to be in a big hurry, but when he saw the young man sitting on the log crying, he stopped, and stared at him.

"'Tut, tut!' he cried. 'What's all this? Who has hurt your feelings?'

" If the young man had not been so sorrowful, he would have been surprised to see the queer-looking little man standing by him. But, as it was, he did n't seem to be surprised at all. He just looked at the stranger with red eyes.

" ' My name is Mum,' said the stranger, ' and I 'm the Man in the Moon. Tell me your troubles. Maybe I can help you. I 'm in a great hurry, because the Moon must change day after to-morrow, and I must be there to lend a hand ; but I 'll not allow my hurry to prevent me from hearing your troubles and helping you if I can.'

" So then and there the young man told his story, and the Man in the Moon sighed heavily when he heard it.

" ' I see how it is,' he said. ' You are young and thoughtless, and your father is old and crabbed. You never thought of what you owed him, and he never made any allowances for your youth. He 's in no danger. I know old Stuff well. I 've watched him many a night when he thought nobody had an eye on him, and he 's a pretty tough and cunning customer. You must have help if you get your father out of trouble.'

A QUEER LOOKING LITTLE MAN CAME JOGGING ALONG THE
ROAD

"'What am I to do?' asked the young man.

"'Well,' replied the Man in the Moon, 'in the first place you will have to go home. Say nothing about the trouble your father is in. Just tell your mother that he has lost the sole of his shoe, and has sent you for the awl that is in the big red cupboard, a piece of leather, a handful of pegs, and a piece of wax.'

"'What then?' the young man inquired.

"'Bring them here,' said the Man in the Moon. 'By the time you get back, I will have another holiday. We'll put our heads together and see what can be done.'

"The young man made no delay. He was so anxious about his father that he started for home at once. It was a long journey, but he lost no time on the way. He was in rags and tatters when he reached home, but that made no difference to him. He took no time to eat, or to sleep, or to rest, but went to his mother at once, and told her that his father had lost the sole of his shoe, and had sent for the awl that lay in the big red cupboard, a strong piece of leather, a handful of shoe-pegs, and a cake of shoemaker's wax.

" His mother asked him a great many questions, as women will, but all the answer the son would make was that his father had lost the sole of his shoe, and had sent for the awl that lay in the big red cupboard, a strong piece of leather, a handful of shoe-pegs, and a cake of shoemaker's wax. Of course, the mother was very much worried. She finally came to the conclusion that some great calamity had befallen her husband, and she went about crying and wringing her hands, and declaring that they were all ruined; that her husband was dead; and that more than likely he had been murdered by this bad, bad son of hers, who had no other story to tell except to ask for the awl that lay in the big red cupboard, a strong piece of leather, a handful of shoe-pegs, and a cake of shoemaker's wax.

" Now, the good son heard all this, but he said nothing. He just folded his hands and fetched a sigh or two, and seemed to be sorry for everything in general. But while the mother was going about wringing her hands and weeping, and the good son was heaving and fetching his sighs, the other son went to the big red cupboard. There on a shelf he saw the awl sticking in a cake of shoemaker's wax. Near it was a strong piece of leather, and close by was a handful of shoe-pegs. He took these, changed his ragged coat, and started back on his journey.

" Now, although the good son did nothing but sigh and look sorry, he had deep ideas of his own. The reason he was called the good son was because he was so cunning. He thought to himself that now would be a good time to do a fine stroke of business. He knew that his brother had something more on his mind than the awl, the leather, the pegs, and the shoemaker's wax, and he wanted to find out about it. So he ran after his brother to ask him what the real trouble was. He caught up with him a little way beyond the limits of the village, but no satisfaction could he get. Then he began to abuse his brother and to accuse him of all sorts of things.

" But the son, who was trying to get his father out of trouble, paid no attention to this. He went forward on his journey, turning his head neither to the right nor to the left. The good brother (as he was called) followed along after the best he could, being determined to see the end of the business. But somehow it happened that, on the second day, the brother who was going to meet the Man in the Moon was so tired and worn out that he was compelled to crawl under a haystack and go to sleep. In this way the good brother passed him on the road and went forward on his journey, never doubting that the other was just ahead of him. Finally, one day, the good brother grew tired and sat down on a log to rest. He sat there so long that the brother he thought he was following came up. He was very much surprised to see his nice and good brother sitting on a log and nodding in that country. So he woke him up and asked him what the trouble was.

"'Stuff!' cried the other, 'you know you have made way with our father!'

"At once there was a roaring noise in the woods and a rustling sound in the underbrush, and out came an old man with a long beard, followed by an army of dwarfs.

"'How dare you abuse me in my own kingdom?' he cried to the good brother. 'How did I ever harm you?'

"The brother, who had seen this game played before, tried to explain, but King Stuff would listen to no explanation. He commanded his armed dwarfs to seize and bind the good brother, and they soon carried him out of sight in spite of his cries.

" Now, the young man who had gone home for the awl and the axe and the shoemaker's wax was very much puzzled. He had more business on his hands than he knew what to do with. He saw that he must now rescue his brother as well as his father, and he did n't know how to go about it. He had the awl and the axe and the shoemaker's wax. He also had the shoe-pegs and leather that he found together. But what was he to do with them? He sat on the log and thought about it a long time.

" While he was sitting there, and just as he was about to go forward on his journey, he heard some one coming briskly down the road singing. He heard enough of the song to be very much interested in it. It ran thus : —

> " ' With the awl and the axe
> And the shoemaker's wax,
> And the pegs and the leather
> That were found close together
>   Where the old man had fling'd 'em,
> We 'll bore through and roar through ;

> We 'll cut down, we 'll put down,
> This king and his kingdom.'

"Of course, it was the Man in the Moon who was coming along the road singing the song, and he seemed to be in high good humor. He caught sight of the solemn face of the young man and began to laugh.

"'There you are!' cried Mum, the Man in the Moon, 'and I 'm glad to see you; but I 'd feel a great deal better if you did n't look so lonesome. I don't know what to do about it. Your face is as long as a hind quarter of beef.'

"'I can't help it,' replied the young man. 'I am in deeper trouble than ever. My brother has been carried off by the same people that captured my father.'

"'What of it?' exclaimed the Man in the Moon. 'If you knew as much about that brother of yours as I do, you 'd go on about your business, and let him stay where he is.'

"'No,' said the young man. 'I could n't do that. I know he is my brother, and that is enough. And then there 's my father.'

"The Man in the Moon looked at the young man a long time, and finally said : —

" 'Since we are to have a sort of holiday together, maybe you won't mind telling me your name.'

" ' Why, of course not,' replied the young man. ' My name is Smat.'

" The Man in the Moon scratched his head and then laughed. ' It is a queer name,' he said; ' but I see no objection to it. I suppose it just happened so.'

" ' Now, I can't tell you anything about that,' replied Smat. ' I was too young when the name was given to take any part in the performance. They seized me, and named me at a time when I had to take any name that they chose to give me. They named me Smat, and that was the end of it so far as I was concerned. They never asked me how I liked it, but just slapped the name in my face, as you may say, and left it there.'

" ' Well,' said the Man in the Moon, ' they 'll put another letter in the name when you get back home. Instead of calling you Smat, they 'll say you are Smart, and there 's some consolation in that.'

" 'Not much as I can see,' remarked Smat. 'It 's all in your mouth, and what is in your mouth is pretty much all wind and water, if you try to spit it out. What I want now is to get my father and my brother out of the trouble that my mischief has plunged them in. Please help me. They ought to be at home right now. There's the corn to grind, and the cows are wait·ing to be milked, and the grain is to be gathered. Times are pretty hard at our house when every·body is away.'

" ' Very well,' said the Man in the Moon. He had hanging by his side the horn of the new Moon, and on this he blew a loud blast. Im·mediately there was a roaring noise in the woods, and very soon there swarmed about them a com·pany of little men, all bearing the tiniest and the prettiest lanterns that were ever seen. It was not night, but their lanterns were blazing, and as they marched around the Man in the Moon in regu·lar order, it seemed as though the light of their lanterns had quenched that of the sun, so that Smat saw the woods in a different light alto·gether. He had not moved, but he seemed to be in another country entirely. The trees had changed, and the ground itself. He was no longer sitting on a log by the side of the big road, but was now standing on his feet in a strange country, as it seemed to him.

" He had risen from his seat on the log when the little men with their lanterns began marching around, but otherwise he had not moved. And yet here he was in a country that was new to him. He rubbed his eyes in a dazed way, and when he opened them again, another change had taken place. Neither he nor the Man in the Moon had made any movement away from the big road and the log that was lying by the side of it, but now they were down in a wide valley, that stretched as far as the eye could see, between two high mountain ranges.

" ' Now, then,' said the Man in the Moon, ' you must be set up in business. On the side of the mountain yonder is the palace of King Stuff, and somewhere not far away you will find your father and your brother, and perhaps some one else.'

" He then called to the leaders of the little men with the lanterns, and gave each one a task to do. Their names were Drift and Sift, Glimmer and Gleam, and Shimmer and Sheen. These six leaders waved their lanterns about, called their followers about them, and at once began to build a house."

"And they so little, too," remarked Mrs. Meadows sympathetically.

"Why, it was no trouble in the world to them," said Little Mr. Thimblefinger. "It did n't seem as if they were building a house. Did you ever see a flower open? You look at it one minute, turn your head away and forget about it, and the next time you look, there it is open wide. That was the way with this house the little men built. It just seemed to grow out of the ground. As it grew, the little men climbed on it, waved their lanterns about, and the house continued to grow higher and higher, and larger and larger, until it was finished. Not a nail had been driven, not a board had been rived, not a plank had been planed, not a sill had been hewn, not a brick had been burned. And yet there was the house all new and fine, with a big chimney-stack in the middle.

"'Now,' said the Man in the Moon, when everything was done, 'here is your house, and you may move in with bag and baggage.'

"'That is quickly done,' replied Smat. 'What then?'

"'Why, you must set up as a shoemaker,' said the Man in the Moon.

"'But I never made a shoe in my life,' the young man declared.

"'So much the more reason why you should make 'em before you die,' the Man in the Moon remarked. 'The sooner you begin to make shoes, the sooner you 'll learn how.'

"'That 's so true,' said Smat, 'that I have no reply to make. 'I 'll do as you say, if I can.'

"'That 's better,' cried the Man in the Moon. 'If you do that, you 'll have small trouble. If you don't, I would n't like to tell you what will happen. Now listen! There is in this kingdom a person (I 'll not say who) that goes about with only one shoe. When you see that person, no matter when or where, — no matter whether it 's man, woman, or child, — you must let it be known that you are ready to make a shoe.'

"Then the Man in the Moon called to the leaders of his army of lantern bearers, and waved his hands. They, in turn, waved their tiny lanterns, and in a moment all were out of sight, and Smat was left alone. For some time afterwards he felt both lonely and uneasy, but this feeling passed away as soon as he went into his house. He was so astonished by what he saw in there that he forgot to feel uneasy. He saw that, although the house was newly built, — if it had been built, — it was in fact old enough inside to seem like home. Every room was finely furnished and carpeted, and in one part of the house, in a sort of shed-room, he found that a shoemaker's shop had been fixed up. There he saw the awl and the axe, and the shoemaker's wax, with the pegs and the leather that were found close together.

" He thought to himself that all that was very nice, but he knew, too, that he was not much of a shoemaker, and this bothered him not a little. Anyhow, he made himself comfortable and waited to see what was going to happen.

"One day a head officer of the kingdom chanced to pass that way. He saw the house and rubbed his eyes. He was so astonished that he went and told another officer, and this officer told another, and finally all the officers in the kingdom knew about it. Now, if you 've ever noticed, those who hold government offices have less to do and more time to do it in than any other day laborers. So they went about and caucussed among themselves, and examined into the books, and found that no taxes had ever been gathered from the owner of such a house. There was great commotion among them. One of them, more meddlesome than the rest, took a big book under his arm and went to Smat's house to make inquiries. The first question he asked was the last.

" Says he, ' How long have you been living in this precinct ? '

" Says Smat, ' Ever since the house was built and a little while before.'

" The officer looked at the house and saw that it was a very old one, and then he tucked his big book under his arm and went off home. At last the king — the same King Stuff whose name you 've heard me mention — heard about the new house that was old, and of the shoemaker who did n't know how to make shoes. So he concluded to look into the matter. He summoned his high and mighty men, and when they had gathered together they went into a back room of the palace and shut the door, and had a long talk together. All this took time; and while the

king and his high and mighty men were confab-
bing together, other things were happening, as
you shall presently see.

"It seems that in that kingdom there was a
beautiful girl who went wandering about the
country. If she had any kinsfolk, nobody knew
anything about it, and, indeed, nobody cared.
She had lost one of her shoes, and she went about
from place to place hunting for it. Some pitied
her, and some laughed at her, which is the way
of the world, as you 'll find out; but nobody
tried to help her. Some said that one shoe was
better than no shoe, and others said that a new
shoe would do just as well as an old shoe."

"That 's where they made a big mistake," said
Mrs. Meadows. "I 've tried it, and I ought to
know. A new shoe is bound to hurt you a little
at first, I don't care how well it fits."

"Well, I 'm only telling you what they said,"
replied little Mr. Thimblefinger. "From all I
can hear, new shoes hurt the ladies a great deal
worse than they do the men. But that 's natural,
for their toes and their heels are a good deal
tenderer than those of the men folks. Anyhow,
this beautiful girl had lost one of her shoes, and,

rather than buy another one or a new pair, she went hunting it everywhere. One day she came by Smat's house. He, sitting by one of the windows, and wishing that he could see his father and brother, paid no attention to the passers-by. But this beautiful girl saw him at the window and spoke to him.

" ' Kind sir,' she said, ' have you seen anything of a stray shoe? I have lost one of mine, and I 'm in great trouble about it.'

" Smat looked at the girl, and she was so beautiful that he could n't help but blush. Seeing this, the girl began to blush. And so there they were, two young things a-blushing at one another, and wondering what was the matter.

" ' I have seen no stray shoe,' said Smat ; ' but if you 'll come in and show me the one you have on, I think I 'll know its fellow when I see it.'

" The girl went into the house and sat on a chair, and showed Smat the shoe that she had n't lost. She had the smallest and the neatest foot he had ever seen.

" ' I hope you are no kin to Cinderella,' said Smat, ' for then you could n't get a shoe to fit your other foot until some kind fairy made it.'

"'I never heard of Cinderella,' the girl replied. 'I only know that I have lost my shoe, and I 'm afraid I 'll never get another just like it.'

"Smat scratched his head, and then he thought about the awl and the axe and the shoemaker's wax, and the pegs and the leather that were found close together. So he said to the beautiful girl :—

"'Just sit here a little while, and I 'll see if I can't get you a shoe to fit your foot. But I must have the other shoe as a pattern to work by.'

"At first the girl did n't want to trust him with the shoe, but she saw that he was in earnest, and so she pulled off the only shoe she had and placed it in Smat's hands. He saw at once that the leather he had was a match for that in the shoe, and he set to work with a light heart,— with a light heart, but his hand was heavy. And yet, somehow or other, he found that he knew all about making shoes, although he had never learned how. The leather fitted itself to the last, and everything went smoothly. But the beautiful girl, instead of feeling happy that she would soon have a mate to her shoe, began to grow sad. She sat in a corner with her head

"HAVE YOU SEEN ANYTHING OF A STRAY SHOE?"

between her hands and her hair hanging down to her feet, and sighed every time Smat bored a hole in the leather with his awl or drove in a peg. Finally, when he handed her the shoe entirely finished, she looked at it, sighed, and let it fall from her hands.

"'Of course,' said Smat, 'I don't feel bad over a little thing like that. But you don't have to pay anything for the shoe, and you don't have to wear it unless you want to.'

"'Oh, it is not that,' cried the beautiful girl. 'The shoe will do very well, but the moment I put it on, your troubles will begin.'

"'Well,' replied Smat, 'we must have troubles of some sort anyhow, and the sooner they begin, the sooner they'll be ended. So put on your shoe.'

"Now, it happened that just as the girl put on the shoe, which fitted her foot exactly, King Stuff and his councilors came driving up to the door. King Stuff was not a large man, but he was very fierce-looking. He called out from his carriage of state and asked what sort of a person lived in that house that he could n't come out and salute when the king and his councilors went riding by. Smat went to the door and bowed as politely as he could, and said that he would have been glad to bow and salute, if he had known his royal highness and their excellent excellencies intended to honor his poor house even so much as to pass by it. The king and his councilors looked at one another and shook their heads.

"'This man is none of us,' said the oldest and wisest of the councilors. 'We must be careful.'

"'How long have you lived here?' asked the king.

"'Longer than I wanted to,' replied Smat. 'My house is so far from the palace that I have not been able to call and pay my respects to your majesty.'

"'I see you are a maker of shoes,' remarked the king, seeing the awl in Smat's hand.

"'No, your majesty, not a maker of shoes, but simply a shoemaker. Thus far I have succeeded in making only one shoe.'

"At this the king and his councilors began to shake and tremble. 'What was the prophecy?' cried the king to the oldest and wisest. 'Repeat it!'

"The oldest and the wisest closed his eyes,

allowed his head to drop to one side, and said in solemn tones : —

> 'Wherever you go, and whatever you do,
> Beware of the man that makes but one shoe ;
> Beware of the man with the awl and the axe,
> With the pegs and the leather and the shoemaker's wax.
> If you 're out of your palace when you meet this man,
> You 'd better get back as fast as you can.'

"Smat felt very much like laughing at the solemn way in which the oldest and wisest councilor repeated this prophecy, or whatever it might be called. 'Your majesty need n't be worried about that prophecy,' said he. 'It 's the easiest thing in the world to break the force of it.'

"'How?' asked the king.

"'Why, having made one shoe, I 'll go to work and make another,' replied Smat.

"The oldest and wisest of the councilors said that was a pretty good plan, — anyhow, it was worth trying. Smat promised to make another shoe, and have it ready in two days. But this was easier said than done. In the first place, he had used nearly all his leather in making a shoe for the beautiful girl. In the second place, the awl point would n't stay in the handle. In the third place, the pegs split and broke every time he tried to drive them, and the shoemaker's wax would n't stick. Everything went wrong at first and grew worse at last, so that when the king sent his officers for the shoe it was no nearer done than it had been before Smat began.

"The beautiful girl had not gone very far away, and she came every day to see how Smat prospered in making the second shoe. She was watching him when the king's officers came for the shoe, and when she saw them she began to weep. But Smat looked as cheerful as ever, and even began to whistle when the officers knocked at the door.

"'We are in a fix,' said he, 'but we 'll get out of it. Lend me the shoe I made for you. I 'll send that to the king and then get it back again.'

"The girl tried to take the shoe from her foot, but nothing would move it. 'That is a sign,' said Smat, 'that it ought not to come off. I 'll just go to the king myself and tell him the facts in the case. That is the best way.'

"So he gathered the awl and the axe and the shoemaker's wax, and the scraps of leather, and bundled them together. Then he told the officers that he would go with them and carry the shoe himself, so as to be sure that it came safely into the king's hands. They went toward the palace, and Smat noticed, as they went along, that it grew darker and darker as they came nearer to the palace. The officers seemed to notice it too. By the time they reached the palace, it was so dark that Smat had great trouble in keeping up with the officers.

" There was great commotion in the palace. Nobody had ever seen it so dark before except just at the stroke of midnight, when the shadows grow thick and heavy and run together and over everything.

" Now, old King Stuff was a sort of magician himself (as, indeed, he had to be in those times, in order to manage a kingdom properly), and as soon as he saw the great darkness coming on at the wrong time of day, he thought at once of the prophecy in regard to the man who made but one shoe. So he hustled and bustled around the palace, calling for the officers he had sent after the shoe. But nobody had seen them return before the dark began to fall, and after that it was impossible to see them.

"In the midst of it all, the officers, followed by Smat, stumbled into the palace and went groping about from room to room hunting for old King Stuff and his ministers. At last, they heard him grumbling and growling, and felt their way toward him.

"'The shoe! the shoe!' cried King Stuff, when the officers had made themselves known.

"'I have something that will answer just as well,' said Smat.

"'The shoe! give me the shoe!' cried the king.

"'Take this, your majesty,' said Smat, handing him the bundle.

"No sooner had the king's hands touched the bundle than there was a rumbling noise in the air, the building began to shake and totter and crumble away. In the midst of it all some one cried out in a loud voice: —

> 'Wherever you go, and whatever you do,
> Beware of the man that makes but one shoe!'

"In the twinkling of an eye, King Stuff and his army and his palace had disappeared from sight. At the same time the darkness had cleared

away, and Smat saw his father and his brother
standing near, dazed and frightened, and not far
away was the beautiful girl. The father and the
brother were very much astonished when they
found that Smat had been the means of their
rescue. They talked about it until night fell,
and then the Man in the Moon, with his tiny lan-
tern-bearers, came and escorted them to their own
country.

"Now it happened that the beautiful girl was
a princess, the daughter of the king. It fell to
the lot of Smat to take the princess home. Not
long after that the king gave a great festival, to
celebrate the return of his daughter. Smat's
father and brother got close enough to the palace
to see him standing in a large room, where there
was a large crowd of people and music and
flowers. They saw, too, that he was holding the
princess by the hand.

"And so," said little Mr. Thimblefinger, wiping
the perspiration from his forehead, "the story
ended."

XX.

"Phew!" exclaimed Mr. Rabbit, when he was sure that little Mr. Thimblefinger had finished. "That beats anything I ever heard."

"I 'm glad you like it," said Mr. Thimblefinger.

"Oh, hold on there!" protested Mr. Rabbit, "you are going too fast. I never said I liked it. I said it beat any story I ever heard, and so it does, — for length. I did n't know that such a little chap could be so long-winded. It was such a long story that I 've forgotten what the moral ought to be."

"Why, I thought you said you did n't believe much in stories that had morals tacked to them," remarked Mrs. Meadows.

"No doubt I did," replied Mr. Rabbit, — "no doubt I did. But this story was long enough to have a dozen morals cropping out in different places, like dog fennel in a cow pasture."

" Well," said Mr. Thimblefinger, " there was a moral or two in the story, but I did n't call attention to them in the telling, and I 'll not dwell on them now."

" I thought it was a tolerably fair story," said Buster John, yet with a tone of doubt.

" Oh, I thought it was splendid all the way through," said Sweetest Susan.

" There are some stories that are hard to tell," suggested Mrs. Meadows. " They go in such a rambledy-wambledy way that it 's not easy to keep the track of them. I remember I once heard Chickamy Crany Crow trying to repeat a story that she heard the Looking-glass Children tell. I never found head nor tail to it, but I sat and listened almost without shutting my eyes."

" What was the story ? " asked Sweetest Susan.

In reply, Mrs. Meadows said she would call Chickamy Crany Crow, and ask her to tell it. As usual, Chickamy Crany Crow was off at play with Tickle-My-Toes. They both came when Mrs. Meadows called them, and Chickamy Crany Crow, after some persuasion, began to tell the story.

"One day," she said, brushing her hair behind

her ears with her fingers, "I wanted to see the Looking-glass Children. Tickle-My-Toes was off playing by himself, and I was lonesome; so I went to the Looking-glass, whirled it around in its frame, and waited for the children to come out. But they did n't come. I called them, but they made no answer. I went close to the Glass, and looked in. At first, I could n't see anything; but after a while I saw, away off in the Glass, one of the children, — the one they all say looks like me. I called her; but she was so far off in the Glass that she could n't hear me, and, as she had her face turned the other way, she could n't see me.

"After so long a time, she came up to the frame of the Glass, and then stepped out and sat down on the ground. I saw she had been crying.

"Says I, 'Honey, what in the world is the matter?' I always call her Honey when we are by ourselves.

"Says she, 'There 's enough the matter. I 'm e'en about scared to death, and I expect that all the other children in this Looking-glass are either captured, or killed, or scared to death.'

"Says I, 'Why did n't you holler for help?'

"Says she, 'What good would that have done? You all could help us very well on dry land, out here, but how could you have helped us in the Looking-glass, when you can't even get in at the door? I've seen you try to follow us, but you've always failed. You stop at the Glass, and you can't get any farther.'

"Says I, 'You are right about that; but if we outside folks can't get in the Glass to play with you and keep you company, how can anybody or anything get in there to scare you and hurt you?'

"Says she, 'The thing that scared us has been in there all the time. It was born in there, I reckon, but I've never seen it before ; and I tell you right now I never want to see it again.'

"Says I, 'What sort of a thing is it?'

"Says she in a whisper, '*It's the Woog!*'

"'The what?' says I.

"'*The Woog!*' says she.

"Says I, 'It's new to me. I never heard of it before.'

"Says she, 'To hear of it is as close as you want to get to it.'

"Why, I heard of the Woog in my younger

days," remarked Mr. Thimblefinger. "I thought
the thing had gone out of fashion."

"Don't you believe a word of it," said Chickamy Crany Crow. "It's just as much in fashion
now as ever it was, especially at certain seasons of
the year. The little girl in the Looking-glass —
I say little girl, though she's about my size and
shape — told me all about it; and as she lives in
the same country with the Woog, she ought to
know."

"What did she say about it?" asked Buster
John, who had a vague idea that he might some
day be able to organize an expedition to go in
search of the Woog.

"Well," replied Chickamy Crany Crow, "she
said this, — she said that she and the other children were sitting under the shade of a bazzle-
bush in the Looking-glass, telling fairy stories.
It had come her turn to tell a story, and she was
trying to remember the one about the little girl
who had a silk dress made out of a muscadine
skin, when all of a sudden there was a roaring
noise in the bushes near by. While they were
shaking with fright, a most horrible monster came
rushing out, and glared at them, growling all the

A HORRIBLE MONSTER GLARED AT THEM

while. It wore great green goggles. Its hair stood out from its head on all sides, except in the bald place on top, and its ears stuck out as big as the wings of a buzzard.

"'Do you know who I am?' it growled. 'No, you don't; but I 'll show you. I am the Woog. Do you hear that? The Woog! Don't forget that. What did I hear you talking about just now? You were talking about fairies. Don't say you were n't, for I heard you.'

"'Well,' says one of the Looking-glass Children, 'what harm is there in that?'

"'Harm!' screamed the Woog. 'Do you want to defy me? I have caught and killed and crushed and smoked out all the fairies that ever lived on the earth, except a few that have hid themselves in this Looking-glass country. What harm, indeed! — a pretty question to ask me, when I 've spent years and years trying to run down and smother out the whole fairy tribe.'

"The Looking-glass Children," Chickamy Crany Crow continued, " told the Woog that they did n't know there was any harm in the fairies themselves, or in talking about them. The Woog paid no attention to their apologies. He just

stood and glared at them through his green goggles, gnashing his teeth and clenching his hands.

"Says the monster after awhile, 'How dare
any of you wish that you could see a fairy, or
that you had a fairy godmother? What shall I
do with you? I crushed a whole population of
fairies between the lids of this book' (he held
up a big book, opened it, and clapped it together
again so hard that it sounded like some one had
fired off a gun), 'and I 've a great mind to
smash every one of you good-for-nothing children
the same way.'

"You may be sure that by this time the poor
little Looking-glass Children were very much
frightened, especially when they saw that the
Woog was fixing to make an attack on them.
He dropped his big book, and when the children
saw him do this they broke and run : some went
one way and some another. The last they saw of
him, he was rushing through the bushes like a
blind horse, threshing his arms about, and doing
more damage to himself than to anybody else.
But the children had a terrible scare, and if he
has n't made way with some of them it 's not
because he is too good to do it."

"The poor dears!" exclaimed Mrs. Meadows sympathetically.

" Dat ar creetur can't come out 'n dat Lookin'-glass like de yuthers, kin he?" inquired Drusilla, moving about uneasily: " kaze ef he kin, I 'm gwine 'way fum here. I dun seed so many quare doin's an' gwine's on dat I 'll jump an' holler ef anybody pints der finger at me."

" Well, Tar-Baby," replied Mr. Rabbit with some dignity, " he has n't never come out yet. That 's all that can be said in that line. He may come out, but if he does you 'll be in no danger at all. The Woog would never mistake you for a fairy, no matter whether he had his green goggles on or whether he had them off."

" No matter 'bout dat," remarked Drusilla. " I may n't look like no fairy, but I don't want no Woog fer ter be cuttin' up no capers 'roun' me. I tell you dat, an' I don't charge nothin' fer tellin' it. Black folks don't stan' much chance wid dem what knows 'em, let 'lone dem ar Woog an' things what don't know 'em. Ef you all hear 'im comin', des give de word, and I boun' you 'll say ter yo'se'f dat Drusilla got wings. Now you min' dat."

"What does the Woog want to kill the fairies for?" asked Sweetest Susan. "He must be very mean and cruel."

"He's all of that, and more," replied Mrs. Meadows. "The fairies please the children, and give them something beautiful to think about in the day and to dream about at night, and the Woog does n't like that. He hates the fairies because it pleases the children to hear about them, and he hates the children because they like to hear about the fairies."

"Well, I never want to see him until I am big enough to tote a gun," said Buster John. "After that, I don't care how soon I meet him."

"Now," remarked Mr. Rabbit, turning to Mrs. Meadows with a solemn air, "did n't you say that all this about the Woog was a tale, or something of that sort."

"I believe I did," replied Mrs. Meadows. "What about it?"

"Just this," said Mr. Rabbit, — "a tale's a tale, and it never stops until all is told."

"If that's the case, I 've heard some here that overshot the mark," remarked Mrs. Meadows.

"No doubt, no doubt," responded Mr. Rabbit. "But what became of the Woog?"

"I know! I know!" cried Tickle-My-Toes, who had been listening to all that was said about the Woog.

"Very well; let's hear about it," suggested Mr. Rabbit.

"'T aint much," said Tickle-My-Toes modestly. "The chap in the Looking-glass that looks like me, he was the one that fell into the hands or the claws of the Woog. He could have got away with the rest, but a piece of straw was caught between his toes, and it tickled him so that he laughed until he could n't run. He just fell on the ground and rolled over and over, laughing all the time. In this way the Woog caught up with him and grabbed him, and carried him away off in the woods in the Looking-glass country. They were away off in that part of the country where there was no green grass on the ground. There were no green leaves on the trees, no flowers blooming, and no birds singing.

"The Woog carried the little chap that looks like me to that dark place, and nearly scared him to death.

"'You pretend to be something or somebody, do you?—you, a shadow in a glass,' growled the Woog.

"'I 'm what I am,' said the little chap.

"'You are not,' cried the Woog. 'You are nothing. Why do you pretend to be somebody or something?'

"The little chap did n't say anything in reply, because there was nothing to say. There's no use in disputing when you can't help yourself. So the Woog took him and tied him to a dead tree, leaving his big book lying near. There is no telling what would have happened to the little chap; but just as soon as the Woog got out of sight, a strong, tall man, with gray hair combed straight back over his head, suddenly máde his appearance, and untied the cords, and set the little chap free.

"'Don't be frightened,' said the tall man; 'I am the Weeze. I have been hunting the Woog for many a long day, and now I think I 'll put an end to him.'

"Presently the Woog came back growling and grumbling. When he looked up and saw the Weeze, it was too late for him to escape. But he turned and tried to run. Just then the Weeze seized the big book and threw it at the Woog. As it hit him, there was a big explosion, and the Woog and his big book both disappeared.

"The little chap that looks like me," said Tickle-My-Toes, "was telling me about it to-day; and he said that it was n't long after the explosion before the flowers began to bloom in that place, and the birds to sing, and the leaves began to grow on the trees. And after awhile the fairies began to peep out from their hiding-places; and when the little chap came away he could see them playing Ring-Around-Rosy on the green grass.

"It was mighty funny, was n't it?" asked Tickle-My-Toes, in conclusion.

XXI.

"Now I 'm not so mighty certain that that is a real tale after all," said Mr. Rabbit, "although it took two to tell it. There 's something the matter with it somewhere. The running-gear is out of order. I 'm not complaining, because what might suit me might not suit other people. It 's all a matter of taste, as Mrs. Meadows's grandmother said when she wiped her mouth with her apron and kissed the cow."

"Well," remarked Mr. Thimblefinger, "there 's no telling what happens in a Looking-glass when nobody is watching. I 've often wanted to know. The little that I 've heard about the Woog and the Weeze will do me until I can hear more."

"I remember a story that I thought was a very good one when I first heard it," said Mrs. Meadows. "But sometimes a great deal more depends on the time, place, and company than on the stories that are told. I 'm such a poor hand at telling tales that I 'm almost afraid to tell any that I know. I 've heard a great many in my day and time, but the trouble is to pick out them that don't depend on a wink of the eye and a wave of the hand."

" Give us a taste of it, anyhow," suggested Mr. Rabbit. " I 'll do the winking, the Tar-Baby can do the blinking, and Mr. Thimblefinger can wave his hands."

" Well," said Mrs. Meadows, " once upon a time there lived in a country not very far from here a man who had a wife and two children, — a boy and a girl. This was not a large family, but the man was very poor, and he found it a hard matter to get along. He was a farmer, and farming, no matter what they say, depends almost entirely on the weather. Now, this farmer never could get the weather he wanted. One year the Rain would come and drown out his crops, and the next year the Drouth would come and burn them up.

" Matters went from bad to worse, and the farmer and his wife talked of nothing else but the Rain and the Drouth. One year they said they would have made a living but for the

Drouth, and the next they said they would have been very well off but for the Rain. So it went on from year to year until the two children,— the boy and the girl, — grew up large enough to understand what their father and mother were talking about. One year they 'd hear they could have no Sunday clothes and shoes because of the Drouth. The next year they 'd hear they could have no shoes and Sunday clothes because of the Rain.

"All this set them to thinking. The boy was about ten years old and the girl was about nine. One day at their play they began to talk as they had heard their father and mother talk. It was early in the spring, and their father was even then ploughing and preparing his fields for planting another crop.

"'We will have warm shoes and good clothes next winter if the Rain does n't come and stay too long,' said the boy.

"'Yes,' replied the girl, 'and we 'll have good clothes and warm shoes if the Drouth does n't come and stay too long.'

"'I wonder why they 've got such a spite against us,' remarked the boy.

"'I'm sure I don't know,' replied the girl. 'If we go and see them, and tell them who we are, and beg them not to make us so cold and hungry when the ice grows in the ponds and on the trees, maybe they'll take pity on us.'

"This plan pleased the boy, and the two children continued to talk it over, until finally they agreed to go in search of the Rain and the Drouth. 'Do you,' said the boy, 'go in search of Brother Drouth, and I will go in search of Uncle Rain. When we have found them, we must ask them to visit our father's house and farm, and see the trouble and ruin they have caused.'

"To this the girl agreed; and early the next morning, after eating a piece of corn bread, which was all they had for breakfast, they started on their journey, the boy going to the east and the girl to the south. The boy traveled a long way, and for many days. Sometimes he thought he would never come to the end of his journey, but finally he came to Cousin Mist's house, and there he inquired his way.

"'What do you want with Uncle Rain?' asked Cousin Mist. 'He is holding court now, and he

is very busy. Besides, you are not dressed
properly. When people go to court, they have
to wear a certain kind of dress. In your case,
you ought to have a big umbrella and an oil-
cloth overcoat.'

"'Well,' replied the boy, 'I have n't got 'em,
and that 's the end of that part of it. If you 'll
show me the way to Uncle Rain's house, I 'll go
on and be much obliged to boot.'

"Cousin Mist looked at the boy and laughed.
'You are a bold lad,' he said, 'and since you are
so bold, I 'll lend you an umbrella and an oil-
cloth overcoat, and go a part of the way with
you.'

"So the boy put on the overcoat and hoisted
the umbrella, and trudged along the muddy road
toward the house of Uncle Rain. When they
came in sight of it, Cousin Mist pointed it out,
told the boy good-by, and then went drizzling
back home. The boy went forward boldly, and
knocked at the door of Uncle Rain's house.

"'Who is there?' inquired Uncle Rain in a
hoarse and wheezy voice. He seemed to have the
asthma, the choking quinsy, and the croup, all
at the same time.

" 'It 's only me,' said the boy.   ' Please, Uncle Rain, open the door.'

" With that, Uncle Rain opened the door and invited the little fellow in.   He did more than that : he went to the closet and got out a dry spot, and told the boy to make himself as comfortable as he could."

" Got out a — what ? " asked Buster John, trying hard to keep from laughing.

" A dry spot," replied Mrs. Meadows solemnly. " Uncle Rain went to the closet and got out a dry spot.   Of course," she continued, " Uncle Rain had to keep a supply of dry spots on hand, so as to make his visitors comfortable.   It 's a great thing to be polite.   Well, the boy sat on the dry spot, and, after some remarks about the weather, Uncle Rain asked him why he had come so far over the rough roads.   Then the boy told Uncle Rain the whole story about how poor his father was, and how he had been made poorer year after year, first by Brother Drouth and then by Uncle Rain.   And then he told how he and his little sister had to go without shoes and wear thin clothes in cold weather, all because the crops were ruined year after year, either by Brother Drouth or Uncle Rain.

" He told his story so simply and with so much feeling that Uncle Rain was compelled to wipe his eyes on a corner of the fog that hung on the towel rack behind the door. He asked the boy a great many questions about his father and his mother.

" 'I reckon,' said Uncle Rain finally, 'that I have done all of you a great deal of damage without knowing it, but I think I can pay it back. Bring the dry spot with you, and come with me.' He went into the barnyard, and the boy followed. They went into the barn, and there the boy saw, tied by a silver cord, a little black sheep. It was very small, but seemed to be full grown, because it had long horns that curled round and round on the sides of its head. And, although the horns were long and hard, the little sheep was very friendly. It rubbed its head softly against the boy's hand, and seemed to be fond of him at first sight.

" Uncle Rain untied the silver cord, and placed the loose end in the boy's hand. 'Here is a sheep,' he said, 'that is worth more than all the flocks in the world. When you want gold, all you have to do is to press the golden spring

THE BOY TOLD UNCLE RAIN THE WHOLE STORY

under the left horn. The horn will then come off, and you will find it full of gold. When you want silver, press the silver spring under the right horn. The horn will come off, and you will find it full of silver. When the horns have been emptied, place them back where they belong. This may be done once, twice, or fifty times a day.'

"The boy did n't know how to thank Uncle Rain enough for this wonderful gift. He was so anxious to get home that he would have started off at once.

"'Wait a minute,' said Uncle Rain. 'You may tell your father about this, but he must tell no one else. The moment the secret of the sheep is told outside your family, it will no longer be valuable to you.'

"The boy thanked Uncle Rain again, and started home, leading his wonderful sheep, which trotted along after him, as if it were glad to go along. The boy went home much faster than he had gone away, and it was not long before he reached there."

"But what became of the little girl?" asked Sweetest Susan, as Mrs. Meadows paused a moment.

"I am coming to her now," said Mrs. Meadows. "The girl, according to the bargain that had been made between her and her brother, was to visit Brother Drouth, and lay her complaints before him. So she started on her way. As she went along, the roads began to get drier and drier, and the grass on the ground and the leaves on the trees began to look as if they had been sprinkled with yellow powder. By these signs, the girl knew that she was not far from the house of Cousin Dust, and presently she saw it in the distance. She went to the door, which was open, and inquired the way to Brother Drouth's. Cousin Dust was much surprised to see a little girl at his door; but, after a long fit of coughing, he recovered himself, and told her that she was now in Brother Drouth's country.

"'If you 'll show me the way,' said the girl, 'I 'll be more than obliged to you.'

"'I 'll go a part of the way with you,' said Cousin Dust, 'and lend you a fan besides.'

"So they went along until they came in sight of Brother Drouth's house, and then Cousin Dust went eddying back home in the shape of a small whirlwind. The girl went to Brother Drouth's door and knocked. Brother Drouth came at once and opened the door, and invited her in.

"' I 'll not deny that I 'm surprised,' said he, ' for I never expected to find a little girl knocking at my door at this time of day. But you are welcome. I 'm glad to see you. You must have come a long journey, for you look hot.'

" With that he went to the cupboard and got her a cool place to sit on, and this she found very comfortable. But still Brother Drouth was n't satisfied. As his visitor was a little girl, he wanted to be extra polite, and so he went to his private closet and brought her a fresh breeze with a handle to it; and, as the cool place had a cushioned back and the fresh breeze a handle that the girl could manage, she felt better in Brother Drouth's house than she had at any time during her long journey. She sat there on the cool place and fanned with the fresh breeze, and Brother Drouth sat in his big armchair and smiled at her. The little girl noticed this after awhile, and so she said : —

"' Oh, you can laugh, but it 's no laughing matter. If you could see the trouble you 've caused at our house, you 'd laugh on the other side of your mouth.'

"When he heard this, Brother Drouth at once became very serious, and apologized. He said he was n't laughing, but just smiling because he thought she was enjoying herself.

"'I may be enjoying myself now,' said the little girl, 'and I 'm much obliged to you; but if I was at home, I should n't be enjoying myself.'

"Then she went on to tell Brother Drouth how her father's crops had been ruined year after year, either by Uncle Rain or by Brother Drouth, and how the family got poorer and poorer all the time on that account, so that the little children could n't have warm shoes and thick clothes in cold weather, but had to go barefooted and wear rags. Brother Drouth listened with all his ears; and when the little girl had told her story, he shook his head, and said that he was to blame as well as Uncle Rain. He explained that, for many years, there had been a trial of strength going on between him and Uncle Rain, and they had become so much interested in overcoming each other that they had paid no attention to poor people's crops. He said he was very sorry that he had taken part in any such affair. Then he told the little girl that he thought he could pay her back for a part of the damage he had done, and that he would be more than glad to do so.

"Says he, 'Bring your cool place and your fresh breeze with you, and come with me.'

"She followed Brother Drouth out into the barnyard, and into the barn; and there, tied by a golden cord, she saw a snow-white goat.

"'This goat,' said Brother Drouth, 'is worth more than all the goats in the world, tame or wild.' With that he untied the golden cord, and placed the loose end in the girl's hand. The goat was small, but seemed to be old; for its horns, which were of the color of ivory, curved upward and over its back. They were so long that, by turning its head a bit, the snow-white goat could scratch itself on its ham. And though it seemed to be old, it was very gentle; for it rubbed its nose and face against the little girl's frock, and appeared to be very glad to see her.

"'Now then,' said Brother Drouth, 'this goat is yours. Take it, and take care of it. On the under side of each horn, you will find a small spring. Touch it, and the horn will come off;

and each horn, no matter how many times you touch the spring, you will always find full of gold and silver. But this is not all. At each change of the moon, you will find the right horn full of diamonds, and the left horn full of pearls. Now listen to me. You may tell your father about this treasure; but as soon as the secret is told out of the family, your goat will be worth no more to you than any other goat.'

"The little girl thanked Brother Drouth until he would allow her to thank him no more. She would have left the cool place and the fresh breeze, but Brother Drouth said she was welcome to both of them. 'When the weather is cold,' said he, ' you can put them away; but when it is warm, you will find that the cool place and the fresh breeze will come in right handy.'

"Thanking Brother Drouth again and again, the girl started on her journey home, leading her wonderful goat, and carrying with her the cool place and the fresh breeze. In this way, she made the long journey with ease and comfort, and came to her father's house without any trouble. She reached the gate, too, just as her brother did. They were very glad to see each other, and the sheep and the goat appeared to be old friends ; for they rubbed their noses together in friendly fashion.

" ' I 'll make our father and mother rich,' said the boy proudly.

" ' And I 'll make them richer,' said the girl still more proudly.

" So they took their wonderful goat and sheep into the stable, gave them some hay to eat, and then went into the house."

XXII.

THE SNOW-WHITE GOAT AND THE COAL-BLACK SHEEP.

"Please don't say that is the end of the story," said Sweetest Susan, as Mrs. Meadows made a longer pause than usual.

"Well, it ought to be the end," replied Mrs. Meadows. "The two children had come home with treasure and riches enough to suit anybody. That ought to be the end of the story. You ought to be able to say that they all lived happily together forever after. That's the way they put it down in the books; but this is not a book story, and so we'll have to stick to the facts.

"Now, then, when the boy and the girl returned home, one with the wonderful sheep and the other with the wonderful goat, they found their father and mother in a great state of mind. The whole country round about had been searched for the children. The mother was sure they had been stolen and carried off. The father, who had his own miseries always in mind, was sure that they had grown tired of the poverty that surrounded them, and had run away to see if they could n't do better among strangers.

"So, when the children had returned home, as happy as larks, their mother fell to weeping, and cried out: ' I am so glad you have escaped, my pretty dears.' The father grinned and said: ' Why do you come back? Is it because the fare elsewhere is no better than it is here ? '

" Now, of course, the children did n't know what to make of all this. They stood with their fingers in their mouths, and wondered what the trouble was. Then they were compelled to answer a shower of questions; and by the time the inquiries had come to an end, they were not feeling very comfortable at all. Finally the boy said : —

" ' My sister and myself were tired of wearing ragged clothes and having little to eat, and so we concluded to seek our fortunes. We knew that Uncle Rain and Brother Drouth had caused all the trouble, and so we thought the best way to do would be to hunt them up and tell them the trouble they were causing to one poor family. I went to see Uncle Rain, and my sister went to see Brother Drouth. We found them at home, and both were in good humor. Uncle Rain gave me a coal-black sheep, and Brother Drouth gave my sister a snow-white goat, and told us that with these we could make our fortunes.'

"'A likely story — a very likely story indeed!' exclaimed the father. 'If you have brought the sheep and the goat home, you would do well to take them back where you got them, else we shall all be put in jail for stealing and for harboring stolen property.'

"'Now don't talk that way to your own children,' said the tender-hearted mother. 'For my part, I believe every word they say;' then she kissed them, and hugged them, and cried over them a little, while the father sat by, looking sour and glum. The children, when they placed the goat and the sheep in the stable, had each taken a handful of gold and silver coins from the horns of the wonderful animals. So now the boy went forward and placed upon the table near his father a handful of gold and silver. The girl did the same.

" The father heard the rattle and jingle of coin, and, looking around, saw there at his elbow more money than he had ever seen before in all his life. He was both astonished and alarmed.

" ' Worse and worse ! ' he cried, throwing up his hands. ' Worse and worse ! We are ruined ! Tell me where you got that treasure, that I may take it back to its owner. Make haste ! If there 's any delay about it, we shall all be thrown into prison.'

" ' Come with us,' said the boy, ' and we will show you where we found the treasure.'

" So they went out of the house and into the stable, and there the children showed their father where the treasure came from.

" ' Wonderful ! most wonderful ! ' exclaimed the father. ' Wonderful! most wonderful!' cried the mother. Then they hugged and kissed their children again and again, and all were very happy. It made no difference now whether crops were good or bad."

" The man was mighty honest," remarked Mr. Rabbit.

" Yes," said Mrs. Meadows. " But a man can be honest and thick-headed at the same time, and

that was the way with this man. He was too
honest to keep other people's money, and too
thick-headed to know how to keep his own."

" Excuse me ! " exclaimed Mr. Rabbit, with a
bow that made his ears flop; " excuse me! I
thought the story had come to an end. You said
they were all very happy ; so I says to myself,
' Now is the time to make a slight remark.' "

" No ; the end of the story is yet to come,"
replied Mrs. Meadows. " But if these children are
getting tired, I 'm ready to quit. Goodness
knows, I don't want to worry them, and I don't
want to make them think that I want to do all the
talking."

" Please go on," said Sweetest Susan.

" Well, when the father found where the
money and treasure came from, he was willing to
believe that his children had visited Uncle Rain
and Brother Drouth; for he knew perfectly well
that the wonderful black sheep and the wonderful snow-white goat were not bred on any farm in
that country. So his mind was easy ; and, as I
said, the father, the mother, and the two children
were all happy together.

" The mother and the children were so happy

that they stayed at home and enjoyed one another's company, and the father was so happy that it made him restless in the mind. He got in the habit of going to the tavern every day, and sometimes more than once a day; and he got to drinking more ale and wine than was good for him. And on these occasions his legs would wobble under him, as if one leg wanted to go home, and the other wanted to go back to the tavern.

"Sometimes, at the tavern, he would get to gaming; and when he lost his money, as he always did, he'd ask his companions to wait until he could go home and get more. He would soon come back with his pockets full. This happened so often that people began to talk about it, and to wonder how a man who had been so very poor could suddenly become so wealthy that he had money to throw away at the gaming-table. His neighbors were very curious about it, but they asked him no questions, and he went on drinking and gambling for many long days.

"But finally there came to that village a company of five men, who let it be understood that they were peddlers. They came into the village on foot, carrying packs on their backs, and put up at the tavern. They were not peddlers, but robbers, who had been attracted to the village by rumors about the poor man who was rich enough to throw away money night after night at the gaming-table.

" Shortly after nightfall, three of the five men arranged themselves around a table; and when the man came in, they invited him to join them. Two of the five sat by the fire, and appeared to be watching the game. The man did n't wait for two invitations, but seated himself at the table, and called for wine. Then the gaming began. Aided by their two companions, the three robbers at the table had no difficulty in swindling the man. Though he came with all his pockets filled with gold and silver, they were soon emptied. The robbers plied him with wine, and he played wildly.

" When his money was all gone, he excused himself and said he would go and get more, and then continue the game. He went out; and, at a sign from the leader, the two robbers who had been sitting by the fire, rose and followed him. They had no trouble in doing this, for the man's legs were already getting wobbly. One leg wanted to go home and go to bed, and the other wanted to go back and be stretched out under the table.

"But, though the man's legs were wobbly, his head was pretty clear. He knew his way home, and he knew his way into the stable, where the coal-black sheep and the snow-white goat were housed. The two robbers followed him as closely as they dared, but it was too dark for them to see what he was doing. They knew that he went into the stable, and presently they heard the jingle and clinking of gold and silver, and then he came out with his pockets full.

"They waited until he had gone on toward the tavern and was out of sight. Then they slipped into the yard, and crept into the stable. It was very dark in the stable, but not too dark to see dimly. The two men felt their way along, and soon saw that there were but two stalls in the stable. Each went into a stall, and began to feel around. They expected to find bags of gold and silver stacked around, but they were mistaken. Finally they stooped to feel along the ground; and, as they did so, there was a loud thump in each stall and a yell of pain from both robbers. When they stooped to feel along the ground, the coal-black sheep and the snow-white goat rushed at them, and gave each one a thump that nearly jarred the senses out of him. The robbers rolled over with a howl, and the goat and the sheep thumped them again, and kept on thumping them.

"But at last the robbers managed to escape, though they made a pretty looking sight. Their hats were lost, their clothes were torn and muddy, their heads were bleeding, their eyes were knocked black and blue, and they felt as if there was not a whole bone in their body. They were too frightened to talk, but finally their voices came to them.

"'What was it hit you?' says one.

"'I'm blessed if I know,' says the other. 'What hit you?'

"'Something hard,' says one.

"'What did it look like?'

"'Satan dressed in white, and he had his maul and wedge with him. What did yours look like?'

"'Satan dressed in black, and he had all his

AT LAST THE ROBBERS MANAGED TO ESCAPE

horns and hoofs with him ; and I think he must have struck me one or two licks with his forked tail.'

" They went off to the nearest branch, and bathed themselves the best they could, but even then they made a sorry spectacle. Their heads and faces were still swollen, their eyes were nearly closed, and their clothes were split and ripped from heel to collar. They did n't know where to go. They knew that it would n't do to go back to the tavern and present themselves among the guests, for that would cast suspicion on their companions. Finally, they went outside the village, and hid themselves under a haystack, where they soon fell asleep, and would have slept soundly if their dreams had not been disturbed by visions of a black Satan and a white Satan, both armed with long, hard horns and sharp hoofs.

" All this time, the father of the children, wobbly as he was, sat at the gaming-table with the three robbers. The robbers were waiting for the return of their companions, and at last they became so uneasy that they played loosely, and the man began to win his gold and silver back again.

At last the robbers concluded to go in search of
their companions; and the man went home, carrying with him more gold and silver than he had
ever before brought away from the tavern. The
robbers failed to find their companions until the
next day, and the story they told was so alarm-
ing that the band concluded to leave that part
of the country, at least for awhile.

"But reports and rumors of the great wealth
of the poor farmer continued to travel about, and
finally they came to the ears of a company of
merchants, who were more cunning in their line
of business than the robbers were in theirs. So
these merchants journeyed to the village, and put
up at the tavern. There they soon made the ac-
quaintance of the fortunate farmer who owned
the wonderful coal-black sheep and the wonderful
snow-white goat.

"They talked business with him from the word
go. They wanted him to put his money in all
sorts of schemes that were warranted to double it
in a few months. But the man said he did n't
want his money doubled. He already had as
much as he wanted. He told them that if he
were to sit on the street and throw away a million

dollars a minute for ten years he 'd be just as rich
at the end of that time as he was before he threw
away the first million.

" Of course, the merchants did n't understand
this. Some said the man was crazy, but the
shrewder ones concluded that there must be some
secret behind it all. So they set to work to find
it out. They flattered him in every way. They
made him rich presents for himself, his wife, and
children. For the first time he began to wear
fine clothes and put on airs. The shrewd merchants asked his advice about their own business,
and went about telling everybody what a wise
man he was. They pretended to tell him all their
own business secrets.

" This, of course, pleased the man very much;
and, at last, one day, when he had more wine in
his head than wit, he told his merchant friends
that he made all his gold and silver by shearing a
black sheep and milking a white goat.

" ' Where do you keep these wonderful creatures ? ' one of the merchants asked.

" ' In my stable,' replied the man, — ' in my
stable night and day.'

" The greedy merchants were not long in find·

ing out that the man kept a coal-black sheep and a snow-white-goat in his stable sure enough ; and, after a good deal of persuading and flattering, they got him to consent to bring his coal-black sheep and his snow-white goat to the tavern, so that they might see for themselves how rare and valuable the animals were.

" Well, one night after his wife and children had gone to bed, the man carried the sheep and the goat to the tavern, and showed them to the merchants. They offered him immense sums of money for the animals, but he refused them all. Then they invited him to remain to a banquet which they had prepared. He wanted to carry his sheep and his goat back home, and then return to the banquet ; but the merchants said the table was already spread, and he could tie his wonderful animals in the rear hall, where nobody would bother them.

" Meantime, the merchants had sent out into the country and bought a black sheep and a white goat ; and while some of them were pouring wine down the man's goozle, others were untying the wonderful black sheep and white goat, and putting in their place the animals that had been bought. When the time came for the man to go home, he was so wobbly in the legs and so befuddled in the head that he could n't tell the difference between a sheep and a goat. In fact, he had forgotten all about them, until one of the merchants asked him if he was n't going to take his rare and valuable animals back home.

"The strange sheep and goat were not used to being led about at night by a man with wobbly legs and a befuddled head, and they cut up such queer capers that it was much as the man could do to keep on his feet at all. But, after so long a time, he managed to get them home, and tied them in the stable.

"So far, so good: but the next morning, when the boy and the girl got up betimes and went out to feed their pets, as they were in the habit of doing, they saw at once that something had happened. Their precious pets had been made way with, and these rough, dirty, and mean-looking animals put in their place. One glance was enough to satisfy the children of this, and they set up such a wail that the whole neighborhood was aroused. Even their father stuck his head out of the window and asked what was the matter. His head was still befuddled by the night's banquet, but his alarm sobered him instantly when he heard what his children said. He would n't believe it at first; but when he went out into the stable and saw for himself, he was nearly beside himself with grief. He declared that it was all his fault, and told what he had done the night before.

" He was now as poor as he ever was ; and his wife said she was n't sorry a bit, because he would now have a chance to go to work and an excuse for not hanging around the tavern. But the children begged him to go after their coal-black sheep and their snow-white goat.

" This he promised to do, and he made haste to go to the tavern. The merchants were still there, but they only laughed at him when he asked them for his sheep and his goat. They called on the tavern-keeper to witness that the man had started home with a black sheep and a white goat.

" ' That is true,' said the man, ' and I have them there now. But they are not mine. Some of you ruffians stole mine and put these in their place.'

" The merchants pretended to be very angry at

this, and made as if they would fall on the man with their fists. But he was a stout fellow, and was armed with a stout hickory, and so they merely threatened. But the man failed to get his coal-black sheep and his snow-white goat, and went home full of grief and remorse."

XXIII.

THE BUTTING COW AND THE HITTING STICK.

"I hope that is n't the end of the story," remarked Buster John.

"Well," replied Mr. Rabbit, "we can either cut it off here, or we can carry it on for weeks and weeks."

"Speak for yourself," said Mrs. Meadows; "or, if you want to, you can tell the rest of the story yourself. No doubt you can tell it a great deal better than I can."

"Now you 'll have to excuse me," remarked Mr. Rabbit. "I thought maybe you were getting tired, and wanted to rest. Go on with the tale. I 'm getting old and trembly in the limbs, but I can stand it if the rest can."

"Well," said Mrs. Meadows, turning to Buster John and Sweetest Susan, "the children were very much worried over the loss of the coal-black sheep and the snow-white goat, and they made up their minds to try and get them back. The boy said he would go and ask Uncle Rain's advice, and the girl said she would visit Brother Drouth once more. So they started on their journey, one going east and the other going south.

" They met with no adventure by the way, and, having traveled the road once, they were not long in coming to the end of their journey. The boy found Uncle Rain at home, and told him all about the loss of his beautiful black sheep. Uncle Rain grunted at the news, and looked very solemn

" ' That 's about the way I thought it would be,' said he. 'It takes a mighty strong-minded person to stand prosperity. But you need n't be afraid. Your sheep is not lost. The men who have stolen him can stand great prosperity no better than your father can. They will wrangle among themselves, and they will never take the sheep away from the tavern. But they shall be punished. Come with me.'

" Uncle Rain went out into his barnyard, and the boy followed him. He went to a stall where a black cow was tied. 'This,' said he, 'is the butting cow. You are to take her with you. She will allow no one to come near her but you, and when you give her the word she will run over and knock down whoever and whatever is in sight. She knows the black sheep, too, for they have long been in the barn together. When she begins to low, the black sheep will bleat, and in that way you may know when you have found it. More than that, the cow will give you the most beautiful golden butter that ever was seen.'

"Uncle Rain untied the cow, placed the end of the rope in the boy's hand, and bade him good-by. The boy went back the way he came, the cow following closely and seeming to be eager to go with him.

"The girl, who had taken the road to Brother Drouth's house, arrived there safely and told her trouble. Brother Drouth said he was very sorry about it, but as it was not a thing to weep over, he did n't propose to shed any tears.

"'What's done,' he said, 'can't be undone; but I 'll see that it 's not done over again.' He went to a corner of the room, picked up a walking-stick, and gave it to the little girl. 'We have here,' he said, 'a walking-stick. It is called the hitting stick. Whenever you are in danger, or whenever you want to punish your enemies, you have only to say: "Hit, stick! Stick, hit!" and neither one man nor a hundred can stand up against it. It is not too heavy for you to carry, but if your hands grow tired of carrying it, just say, "Jump, stick!" and the stick will jump along before you or by your side, just as you please.'

"Then Brother Drouth bade the girl good-by; and she went on her way, sometimes carrying the hitting stick, and sometimes making it jump along the road before her.

"Now, then, while all this was going on, the greedy merchants found themselves in a fix. When they first got hold of the coal-black sheep and the snow-white goat, they thought that they had had a good deal of trouble for nothing. But merchants, especially the merchants of those days, when there was not as much trade as there is now, had very sharp eyes, and it was not long before they found the springs under the horns of the sheep and the goat. Having found the treasure, they remembered that the man had spent more money in two days than the horns of the animals would hold, and this led them to discover that the horns were always full of treasure.

"For a little while they were very happy, and congratulated one another many times over. But

in the midst of their enjoyment the thought came
to them that there must be a division of this treasure. The moment the subject was broached, the
wrangle began. There were more than a dozen
of the merchants, and the question was how to
divide the treasure so that each might have an
equal share. Though they took millions from the
horns of the black sheep and the white goat, yet
whoever had the animals would still have the most.

"It was a mighty serious question. They ar-
gued, they reasoned, they disputed, and they wran-
gled, and once or twice they came near having a
pitched battle. But finally, after many days, it
was decided that one party of merchants should
have the black sheep and that another party
should have the white goat. This didn't satisfy
all of them, but it was the best that could be done;
and so they departed, the party with the white
goat going south, and the party with the black
sheep going east.

"Now, a very curious thing happened. If
either party had kept on traveling, it would have
met the boy or the girl; one with the butting cow,
and the other with the hitting stick. But both
parties were dissatisfied; and they had gone but a

little way before they stopped, and after some talk determined to go back. The merchants with the white goat determined to follow on after the merchants that had the black sheep, and secure the animal by fair means or foul. The merchants with the black sheep determined to follow the merchants with the white goat, and buy the animal or seize him. So each party turned back.

"The merchants with the white goat reached the tavern first. They had hardly refreshed themselves, when the tavern-keeper came running in, to tell them that the other merchants were coming.

"'Then take our white goat and hide it in your stable,' they said.

"The landlord did as he was bid; and then meeting the merchants with the black sheep, he told them that their companions of the morning had also returned.

"'Then take our black sheep and hide it in your stable,' they said. This the landlord quickly did, and returned to the tavern in time to hear the merchants greet each other.

"'What are you doing here?' asked the black sheep merchants.

"'We have lost our white goat,' they replied,

'and have come here to hunt it. Why have you returned?'

"'We have come on the same errand,' said the others. 'We have lost our black sheep, and have returned to find it.'

"Now, the tavern-keeper was not a very smart man, but he had no lack of shrewdness and cunning. He had heard the merchants wrangling and quarreling over the black sheep and the white goat, and now he saw them coming back pretending to be hunting for both the animals, though neither one was lost. He had sense enough to see that there must be something very valuable about the black sheep and the white goat; and so, while the merchants were taking their refreshments, each party eyeing the other with suspicion, the tavern-keeper slipped out into his stable, and carried the black sheep and the white goat to an outhouse out of sight and hearing of the guests.

"As for the merchants, they were in a pickle. Neither party wanted to go away and leave the other at the tavern; so they waited and waited, — the black sheep party waiting for the white goat party to go, and the white goat party waiting for the black sheep party to go.

"'When do you leave?' says one.

"'As soon as we find our sheep. When do you leave?' says the other.

"'Quite as soon.'

"There was not much satisfaction in this for either side. Finally, one of the merchants called the tavern-keeper aside, and asked him where he had put the black sheep.

"'In my stable, your honor,' replied the man.

"Then another merchant called the tavern-keeper aside, and asked him where he had put the white goat.

"'In my stable, your honor,' he replied.

"Now as each of these merchants went out to see that his precious animal was safe, it was perfectly natural that they should see each other slipping about in the yard, and that they should meet face to face in the stable. Both made the excuse that they thought they might find their lost animals at that point, and both were terribly worked up when they saw that the stable was empty. Each went back and told his companions, and pretty soon there was the biggest uproar in that house that the tavern-keeper had ever heard.

"Both parties went running to the stable, fall‑ing over each other on the way; but the black sheep and the white goat were gone. Then the merchants went running back into the tavern, and all began yelling at the tavern-keeper. Instead of making any answer, that cunning chap put his fingers in his ears, and politely asked the mer-chants if they wanted to jar the roof off of the house. They danced around him, yelling and shaking their fists at him, but he kept his fingers in his ears.

"Finally, they caught hold of the man, and began to pull and haul him around at a great rate. In this way they compelled him to take his fingers out of his ears; but he could hear little better, for the whole crowd was dancing around and squalling like a lot of crazy people at a picnic. All the tavern-keeper could hear was : —

" ' Where 's our ' — ' You 've got our ' — ' Sheep ! ' ' Goat ! '

"There was more noise than sense to this rip-pit. There was so much noise that it roused the whole neighborhood, and the people of the village came running in to see what the trouble was. Among them was the mayor ; and he succeeded in quieting the rumpus, not because he was mayor, but because he had a louder voice than any of them.

" When everything was quiet, the mayor asked the merchants why they were acting like crazy people.

" ' Because this man has robbed us,' they cried, pointing to the tavern-keeper.

" ' Of what has he robbed you?' asked the mayor.

" ' Of a black sheep and a white goat,' they replied.

" ' Your honor,' said the tavern-keeper, when the mayor had turned to him, ' you have known me all my life, and have never heard that I was a thief. I want to ask these men a few questions.' By this time the two parties of merchants had ranged themselves on different sides of the room. The tavern-keeper turned to the black sheep party. ' Did n't the men over there come into this house and tell you that they had lost their white goat?'

" ' They certainly did,' was the reply.

" Then he turned to the white goat party. ' Did n't the men over there tell you that they had lost their black sheep and had come back to hunt it ? '

" ' They certainly did,' came the answer.

" Both parties tried to explain that they had placed their animals in charge of the tavern-keeper, but while they were hemming and hawing a queer thing happened. The boy had come up with his butting cow; and seeing the merchants still in the tavern, he led her to the door, and told her to do her whole duty, and nothing but her duty.

" While the merchants were trying to explain, the cow rushed into the room with a bellow, her tail curled over her back, and went at the men with head down and horn points up. Tables and chairs were nothing to the butting cow. She ran over them and through them ; and in a little while the room was cleared of the merchants, and some of them were hurt so badly that they could scarcely crawl away.

" The mayor had jumped through a window, and the village people had scattered in all directions. By this time the tavern-keeper, who had remained unhurt, was laughing to himself at the fix the merchants found themselves in, for the butting

"HIT STICK! STICK HIT!" SHE CRIED

cow was still pursuing them. But he laughed too soon. The little girl came to the door with her hitting stick.

" ' Hit, stick ! Stick, hit ! ' she cried ; and in an instant the stick was mauling the tavern-keeper over the head and shoulders and all about the body.

" ' Help ! help ! ' shouted the tavern-keeper. ' Somebody run here ! Help ! I 'll tell you where they are ! I 'll show you where they are ! '

" ' Stop, stick ! ' said the girl. ' Now show me where my snow-white goat is.'

" ' Yes ! ' exclaimed the boy. ' Show me where my coal-black sheep is ! '

" ' Come,' said the tavern-keeper ; and he went as fast as he could to the outhouse where he had hid the animals. They were in there, safe and sound, and the children made haste to carry them home.

" So the farmer was once more rich and prosperous. He shunned the tavern and kept at work, and in this way prosperity brought happiness and content to all the family. And by giving freely to the poor they made others happy too."

XXIV.

THE FATE OF THE DIDDYPAWN.

" It has always been mighty curious to me," said Mr. Rabbit, " why everything and everybody is not contented with what they 've got. There 'd be lots less trouble in the country next door if everybody was satisfied."

" Well," remarked Mr. Thimblefinger, " some people have nothing at all. I hope you don't want a man who has nothing to be satisfied. An empty pocket makes an empty stomach, and an empty stomach has a way of talking so it can be heard."

" That is true," replied Mr. Rabbit; " but there is a living in the world for every creature, if he will only get out of bed and walk about and look for it. But a good many folks and a heap of the animals think that if there is a living in the world for everybody, it ought to be handed round in a silver dish. Then there are some folks and a great many creatures that are not satisfied with what they are, but want to be somebody or something else. That sort of talk puts me in mind of the Diddypawn."

" What is the Diddypawn ? " asked Buster John.

" Well, it would be hard to tell you at this time of day," replied Mr. Rabbit, rubbing his chin thoughtfully. " There are no Diddypawns now, and I don't know that I ever saw but one. He is the chap I 'm going to tell you about. He was a great big strong creature, with a long head and short ears, and eyes that could see in the dark. He had legs that could carry him many a mile in a day, and teeth strong enough to crunch an elephant's hind leg. The Diddypawn would have weeded a wide row if he had been a mind to ; but, instead of doing that, he just lay in the mud on the river bank, and let the sun shine and the rain fall. He had but to reach down in the water to pick up a fish, or up in the bushes to catch a bird.

" But all this did n't make his mind easy. He was n't contented. The thought came to him that a fine large creature such as he was ought to be able to swim as fast as a fish, and fly as high as a bird. So he worried and worried and worried about it, until there was no peace in that neighborhood. All the creatures that crawled, or walked, or swam, or flew, heard of the Diddypawn's troubles. At first they paid no attention to him, but he groaned so long and he groaned so loud that they could n't help but pay attention. They could n't sleep at night, and they could n't have any peace in the daytime.

"For I don't know how long the Diddypawn rolled and tumbled in the mud, and moaned and groaned because he did n't have as many fins as the fishes and as many feathers as the birds. He moaned and mumbled in the daytime, and groaned and grumbled at night. The other creatures paid no attention to him at first; but matters went from bad to worse, and they soon found that they had to do something or leave the country.

"So, after awhile the fishes held a convention, and the porpoise and the catfish made speeches, saying that the Diddypawn was in a peck of trouble, and asking what could be done for him. Finally, after a good deal of talk about one thing and another, the convention of fishes concluded to call on the Diddypawn in a body, and ask him what in the name of goodness he wanted.

" This they did ; and the reply that the Diddypawn made was that he wanted to know how to swim as well as any fish. There was n't anything unreasonable in this ; and so the convention, after a good deal more talk, said that the best way to do would be for every fish to lend the Diddypawn a fin.

" The convention told the Diddypawn about this, and it made him grin from one ear to the other to think that he would be able to swim as fast as the fishes. He rolled from the bank into the shallow water, and the fishes, as good as their word, loaned him each a fin. With these the Diddypawn found he was able to get about in the water right nimbly. He swam around and around, far and near, and finally reached an island where there were some trees.

" ' Don't go too near the land,' says the cat-fish. ' Don't go too near the land,' says the perch.

" ' Don't bother about me,' says the Diddypawn. ' I can walk on the land as well as I can swim in the water.'

" ' But our fins!' says the catfish and the perch. 'If you go on land and let them dry in the sun, they 'll be no good to either us or you.'

" ' No matter,' says the Diddypawn, ' on the land I 'll go, and I 'll be bound the fins will be just as limber after they get dry as they were when they were wet.'

" But the fishes set up such a cry and made such a fuss that the Diddypawn concluded to give them back their fins, while he went on dry land and rested himself. He went on the island, and stretched himself out in the tall grass at the foot of the big trees, and soon fell asleep. When he awoke, the sun was nearly down. He crawled to the waterside, and soon saw that the fishes had all gone away. He had no way of calling them up or of sending them a message, and so there he was.

" While the Diddypawn was lying there wondering how he was going to get back home, he heard a roaring and rustling noise in the air. Looking up, he saw that the sky was nearly black with birds. They came in swarms, in droves, and in flocks. There were big birds and little birds, and all sorts and sizes of birds. The trees on the

IT MADE HIM GRIN FROM EAR TO EAR

island were their roosting-place, but they were coming home earlier than usual, because they wanted to get rid of the moanings and groanings of the Diddypawn.

" The birds came and settled in the trees, and were about to say good-night to one another, when the Diddypawn rolled over, and began to moan and groan and growl and grumble. At once the birds ceased their chattering, and began to listen. Then they knew they would have no sound sleep that night if something was n't done; and so the King-Bird flew down, lit close to the Diddypawn's ear, and asked him what in the name of goodness gracious he was doing there, how he got there, and what the trouble was anyway.

" All the answer the Diddypawn made was to roll over on his other side, and moan and mumble. Once more the King-Bird fluttered in the air, and lit near the Diddypawn's ear, and asked him what in the name of goodness gracious he was doing there, how he got there, and what the trouble was anyway. For answer, the Diddypawn turned on the other side, and groaned and grumbled.

" How long this was kept up I 'll never tell you,

but after a while, the Diddypawn said the trouble with him was that he wanted to fly.   He said he would fly well enough if he only had feathers; but, as it was, he did n't have a feather to his name, or to his hide either.

" Well, the birds held a convention over this situation, and after a good deal of loud talk, it was decided that each bird should lend the Diddypawn a feather.   This was done in the midst of a good deal of fluttering and chattering.   When the Diddypawn was decked out in his feathers, he strutted around and shook his wings at a great rate.

" ' Where shall I fly to ? ' he asked.

" Now, there was another island not far away, on which everything was dead, — the trees, the bushes, the grass, and even the honeysuckle vines. But some of the trees were still standing.   With their lack of leaf and twig they looked like a group of tall, black lighthouses.   When the Diddypawn asked where he should fly, Brother Turkey Buzzard made this remark : —

> " ' If you want to fly fast and not fly far,
>   Fly to the place where the dead trees are ! '

" To this the Diddypawn made reply, —

"'I want to fly fast and not too far,
So I'll fly to the place where the dead trees are!'

"Then the Diddypawn fluttered his feathers and hopped about, and, after a while, took a running start and began to fly. He did n't fly very well at first, being a new hand at the business. He wobbled from side to side, and sometimes it seemed that he was going to fall in the water, but he always caught himself just in time. After a while he reached the island where everything was dead, and landed with a tremendous splash and splutter in the wet marsh grass.

"As dark had not set in, the most of the birds flew along with the Diddypawn, to see how he was going to come out. The Diddypawn had hardly lit, before Brother Turkey Buzzard ups and says:—

"'I don't want my feather to get wet, and so I'll just take it back again.' This was the sign for all the birds. None wanted his feather to get wet, so they just swooped down on the Diddypawn and took their feathers one by one. When the fluttering was over, the Diddypawn had no more feathers than fins. But he made no complaint. He had it in his mind that he'd rest easy during the night and begin his complaints the next morning.

"Says he, 'I've got the birds and the fishes so trained that when I want to fly, all I've got to do is to turn over on my left side and grunt, and when I want to swim, all I've got to do is to turn over on my right side and groan.' Then the Diddypawn smiled, until there were wrinkles in his countenance as deep and as wide as a horse-trough.

"But the birds went back to their roosting-place that night, and there was nothing to disturb them; and the fishes swam around the next day, and there was nothing to bother them.

"Matters went on in this way for several days, and at last some of the birds began to ask about the Diddypawn. 'Had anybody seen him?' or 'Did anybody know how he was getting on?'

"This was passed around among the birds, until at last it came to the ears of Brother Turkey Buzzard. He stretched out his wings and gaped, and said that he had been thinking about taking his family and calling on the Diddypawn. So that very day, Brother Turkey Buzzard, his wife and his children and some of his blood kin, went down to the dead island, to call on the Diddypawn. They went and stayed several days. The rest of the birds, when they came home to roost, could see the Turkey Buzzard family sitting in the dead trees; and after so long a time they came back, and went to roost with the rest of the birds. Some of them asked how the Diddypawn was getting on, and Brother Turkey Buzzard made this reply : —

> " 'The Diddypawn needs neither feather nor fin,
> He 's been falling off, till he 's grown quite thin,
> He has lost all his meat and all of his skin,
> And he needs now a bag to put his bones in.'

" This made Brother Owl hoot a little, but it was n't long before all the birds were fast asleep."

Mr. Rabbit never knew how the children liked the story of the Diddypawn. Buster John was about to say something, but he saw little Mr. Thimblefinger pull out his watch and look up at the bottom of the spring.

" What time is it ? " asked Mrs. Meadows, seeing that Mr. Thimblefinger still held his watch in his hand.

" A quarter to twelve."

"Oh," cried Sweetest Susan, "we promised mamma to be back by dinner time."

"There's plenty of time for that," said Mrs. Meadows. "I do hope you'll come again. It rests me to see you."

The children shook hands all around when Mr. Thimblefinger said he was ready to go, and Mr. Rabbit remarked to Buster John : —

"Don't forget what I told you about Aaron."

There was no danger of that, Buster John said; and then the children followed Mr. Thimblefinger, who led them safely through the spring, and they were soon at home again.